I0569810

THE
HEART CROSSWAYS

James Claffey

THRICE PUBLISHING

Thrice Publishing
PO Box 725114
Roselle, IL 60172
ThricePublishing.com

The Heart Crossways
Copyright ©2018 by James Claffey
JamesClaffey.com
Book Design by David Simmer II and Thrice Arts
Cover Photo by Elizabeth Claffey
Author Photo by Maureen Claffey

First Thrice Publishing Edition: September 2018

ISBN-10: 1-945334-02-9
ISBN-13: 13-978-1-945334-02-3

Printed in the United States of America

To my mother, Elizabeth "Betty" Claffey,
for nurturing my love of reading and writing.

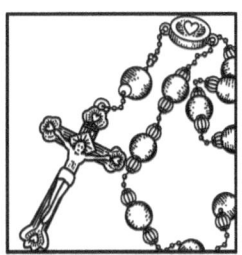

Chapter 1

On rainy days the time passes slowly. Trance-like, I tongue my bedroom window and lick the condensation from the glass. My nose smushes against the cold pane. The seagulls glower below, on the roof of the coal shed, eyes fixed on the kitchen door for the off-chance Mam might throw out some scraps for them to fight over.

Rivulets race down the window at different speeds, my eyes fixed on a favorite. The storm lasts so long I could stare into the garden all day. Instead, I haul the trunk with the crushed lining out of the wardrobe that houses my aunt's mothy fur coat and her cello. Inside the trunk, old notebooks, journals, well-thumbed copies of *Ireland's Own* from the fifties, and at the bottom, an old *Freeman's Journal*—the Great Strike, Larkin, arms outspread, Jesus in a raincoat, the picture hard to make out, the ink smeared and the background fuzzed. The Old Man speaks of "Big Jim" and his impassive dignity, how he fought to overturn the unfair treatment of workers in the dockyards.

From downstairs, the smell of roast lamb wafts through the rungs of the banisters. Mam's bustles about, whacking a chunk of dough with the rolling pin. I'd rather she beat the dough than the backs of my legs, which is often the punishment for refusing to comply with what the teacher says at school, or for not taking the bins out on time.

Sunday.

Mass.

Lamb with mint sauce.

Afternoon—spread manure on the roses.

Evening—a decade of the Rosary.

We kneel to face the wall, the television set cold and brooding behind our backs. Mouth the words. The Hail Marys fall into line, and the Our Father follows. The Hail Holy Queen rounds the evening out. A word out of place, a disruption of the sacred rhythm, and the Old Man stops me in my tracks, clips my ear, and resumes the litany without a hitch.

The Old Man's dismal mood is broken by rare moments of happiness, as it is in the kitchen tonight when he grabs Mam and dances her around faster and faster until she is dizzy.

"Wouldn't it be grand to have a house with a gravel driveway and crystal chandeliers on the ceilings?" he says, and draws Mam to his side and gives her a sloppy kiss. He slaps her bottom and says, "I grew up in a house where even the dogs ate off bone china."

"Get away with you," she says. "It's far from crystal chandeliers you were reared." She snorts, turns the tap on in the sink, and scrubs the dishes.

In the living room, the top of the piano houses the Waterford crystal vases and bowls, the fragile ones at the back, nearest the wall. There was more at one time, but when I was seven my father bungled the family business, a bar and grocery store, away.

Mam says the Old Man's troubles are rooted in the whiskey bottle he used pour from behind the bar of the family business. He manned the bar day and night, a Will's Gold Flake cigarette between his teeth and another one behind his ear, as he served drinks and told stories to his old cronies. Uncle Dermot, who died in the 1970s took handfuls of notes from the cash box and disappeared in a vapor of Jameson's finest, coattails flying, his lazy eye on the lookout for a cute girl.

The money dried to a trickle, and with it his friends. Mam says the bank manager insisted on the title deed until the debts were settled, and the Old Man was never the same again. "A broken man," she says.

Whatever was worth selling got auctioned off. The auctioneer, Mursheen Daly, all rosy cheeks and drunk as a goat, took the lowest offers on everything worth a few quid; at least that's the way the Old Man tells it.

The mere mention of Athleague puts the Old Man in poor twist.

"We left that place and all I had was the boots on my feet," he says.

The impassive bank manager who wouldn't lend him the money to save the business undermined his life forever after. We still own some property outside of the town—a few acres of apple orchard on the Dublin Road. Most of the trees are dead and gnarled, and the ones left bear bitter crab apples.

It's been seven years since we left, and in the spare room we're using for storage there's a large mahogany wardrobe filled with the stuff that didn't sell at auction. I love the silver flask with the large dent in the side. There are flowery letters carved on it and when I asked Mam whose they are, she said to put it back where I found it and never take it out again. I like to finger the initials, FHG, and say them over and over under my breath. The only person with an H in their name in our family is Uncle Harry, and we're hardly allowed to speak about him since we left Athleague. I wish it were different, because he's married to Auntie Martha who makes the best flapjacks, and now we never get to see her at all, and Mam won't use her recipe for fear of upsetting the Old Man.

Mam, the Old Man, Granny and I moved to a terraced, red-bricked Victorian house on a quiet *cul-de-sac* in the Dublin suburbs after the business failed; four bedrooms, kitchen, dining room, sitting room, a fusty attic, and a large back garden with a shed and a greenhouse.

The Old Man spends two weeks away and two weeks at home. He toils with heavy machinery and hard drinkers on the Dunlin Alpha oil-drilling platform in the North Sea. I know he doesn't like the work as an offshore driller, and he'd rather play golf and drink with his friends. Mam says it's backbreaking work, and his body can't take it much more.

When he's home he lingers in the dark, brooding in the sitting room with the curtains drawn shut, nursing a glass of whiskey, the horseracing on the telly. A lot of the time he complains about headaches, and says, "Jesus Christ, this is some pickle we're in now," and we never do any fun things together.

In Athleague, he'd take me for walks by the river and point out the different kinds of birds: wrens, kingfishers, blue tits, and the trees; sycamore, willow, pine, and oak. Now, he neglects me, and all he does is argue with Mam about stupid stuff like money and land and interest rates. The other day I asked if I could help sort his fishing flies out with him and he harrumphed and got mad with me because I spilled some of them on the dining room floor.

A moment of misrule, and on cue, the Old Man metes out the blows. The flat of his hand is weapon enough, the debt scored in red welts on white skin. Why he beats me, I have no idea. Sometimes, the way he looks at me scares me and makes me want to hide in the coal shed forever.

Even all these years later, he's full of fury. He talks about the family business, and curses the banks for the way they held our family to ransom, and when Mam tries to calm him down, he yells at the pair of us, asking whether a man can't express himself in the privacy of his own home. Mam wrinkles her nose at this and that sends him into a greater rage that only goes away when he leaves for the pub.

While he is at sea our lives exist on different planes, two worlds in which the same clock ticks the same time, but without his overpowering menace in the house he might as well be digging trenches on the moon for all I care.

The house thrums with the possibility of another argument that'll see me skitter for the safety of the jacks, or my bedroom, the few sanctuaries I have when the world is in what Mam declares, "a terrible state of chassis." When the walls reverberate from the door slams, I long for a different life. Sometimes anger rolls across his face in tidal waves, sometimes red, sometimes pale, his lips set and fists clench and unclench.

I sit in the sepulchral wardrobe, torch in hand, turn the pages of *The Adventures of Tom Sawyer,* and wish I were afloat on the Mississippi. The wardrobe provides some protection against the ire that washes the house like the gushing of one of his oilrigs. I huddle in the back, knees to my chest. There is a delay between the door slams and the yells. A summons to Our Lord, whose name I am forbidden to take in vain, an appeal to the "Sweet Jesus," the Old Man worships, does me no good. I imagine God as a bitter, angry one who takes delight as he metes out punishment to ordinary sinners. I shut my eyes tight, pray staccato prayers for bolts of lightning to strike the Old Man down, or for him to plunge over the side of the oil platform and perish in the frigid North Sea, or at least for a heart attack to put a stop to his marauding.

The Old Man records my transgressions in a large blue ledger with marbled edges. *Dropped lumps of coal out of the scuttle whilst taking it to the living room fireplace. Punishment:*

six slaps with the leather dog collar. Stealing money from Mam's purse. Punishment: Fifteen slaps with the leather dog collar. Asking too many questions. Punishment: Sent to my room for the afternoon.

Mam maintains the ledger while the Old Man is at sea. He tells her before he goes to sea; "Make sure you write down all his impertinences, his sins, and when I return from the rig I'll deal with him."

His power is unshakeable. My curses, the broken objects, stolen money, all writ in her fine hand, underneath the ancient orders for bricks and wooden planks and the other goods purchased by him when the business thrived.

I stay home from school in case my flu gets worse, but Mam let me go with her to the village shops to buy groceries. She wraps the wool scarf tight about my neck to keep me from getting a chill, her fingers tangled in my too-long hair. She shouts up the stairs to Granny and says we'll be back in a bit. Granny doesn't reply and Mam says, "She must be taking forty winks."

Mam and I go in to check on Granny in her bedroom. She's all bundled up like the Queen of Sheba, as the Old Man likes to say. She smiles at me and the tea cup rattles in her hand as she tries to place it on the nightstand. Then, when Mam says the Old Man has gone out for the morning, Granny says, "That man is full of chat for any dog or devil, but when it comes to his own kin he's a desperate sort altogether. I don't know what possessed you to marry him, at all."

There's hatred in her words, and even though the Old Man's explained why the family business went up in smoke and the bank had to foreclose, Granny blames him for all ills. She sits up in bed, the pillows plumped behind her back, her dark hair flecked with gray, and her eyelashes crusted with sleep. Mam says she looks drawn and Granny snorts at her, wrinkled lines across her forehead. Mam tries to explain the guilt the Old Man feels at how he landed in this predicament, but Granny won't hear any of it and pulls her nightcap down over her ears.

"Well, we're off to the village to do the groceries," Mam says, and tugs the door shut behind us.

Mam tells me, "I feel bad keeping you at home from school, but it's a safety measure."

According to Mam, Uncle Harry nearly died when he was my age. He had scarlet fever and Granny was at her wits end. I'm lucky Mam loves me so much. I don't mind, as I get to have tea with all her friends from the avenue; old ladies with handbags the size of small cars, and mustaches like the Old Man grows when he's on holidays.

The clouds above the Dublin Mountains are singed cotton balls and the branches of the rose bush tremble in the cold October wind she hates so much. The lawn is a muddy square of muck, and the fallen leaves mulch the ragged blades of grass.

We tramp up the Rathgar Road to the shops and pass the orange workman's shelter beside the primary school I don't attend because we're not Protestants. Mam says something about the laborers wasting the taxpayer's money, and how all they do is play cards and sup tea morning, noon, and night.

A blind man taps his white stick against the curb at the traffic lights, and I wonder if there are holes where his eyes should be. She tells me not to stare.

When we get into the Gourmet Shop, she asks the shop-keeper for some brown sugar, the kind with large granules. He smiles and rubs my head, then points out the sugar, which is cramped in a corner behind a basket full of stinky cheeses.

"It's to baste the ham," Mam says.

He nods, and says, "Sure you'll be pleased as punch with a ham covered in that Demerara sugar."

We also buy a tin of Robin's Starch, the one with the little bird on the can. When I ask why she needs it, she says it's so she can iron our dirty underpants, because they look a bit shabby. The Old Man's underpants are huge things, like ship's sails, white and wide. There's a slit where his yoke goes, but my underpants don't have one. Maybe when I'm a bit older.

We stop in at the corner shop across the road from our house before going home. Old Mrs. Dooley is as blind as a turnip and stone deaf, too. She waits behind the counter for the customers to arrive in the morning. Papers, cigarettes, sweets, peat briquettes, cylinders of natural gas, loaves of bread, bottles of salad cream and tomato ketchup, are her domain. She perches on a three-legged stool and passes snide remarks about all and sundry.

She possesses the remarkable ability to mutter curses about a person under her breath, as all the while she wears a simpering smile. With a thick country accent acquired in the ditches of Kerry she blathers about politics, religion, and football all day long. "Oh yes, Kerry will win the All-Ireland again as usual, a strong back line and lightning speed up front. No, the church would never sanction divorce at all, not at all at all." And when talk turns to politics she grinds her teeth, her wrinkled face contorted with disgust, and opines that since Fine Gael's coalition with the Labour Party a few years back nothing has improved, and Fianna Fáil will return to power and set the country to rights at the next election.

Mam is sure she's on the make. She swears up and down that she saw her press a pinkie finger to the weighing scales when she cut slices of corned beef for her one time. "She could peel an orange in her pocket," Mam says, and turns up her nose.

And it is for the most part true; Mrs. Dooley's a woman of penny-pinching ways, always on the lookout for some opportunity to prosper at another's discomfort.

We put everything on tick. The weekly messages are written down in the big red duplicate book and the total totted up each Saturday and paid in full at the end of each month. Mam fixes up with Mrs. Dooley when the Old Man returns home with the pay packet—a brown envelope with the flap sealed and the notes and coins folded inside.

Once a month, Mam traipses across to the dairy, past the Golden's house, and often stops for a cup of tea with Mrs. Golden before she pays the outstanding balance. The religious nature of her monthly settling of accounts is carved in stone. Nothing diverts her from her duty, the careful way she tallies the pound notes and the pennies, and pays her dues. Mam says, "All you have in this life is your good name."

I'm on the floor in front of the fire reading about an infestation of cockroaches in a grain storage facility in County Cork. Out the window I see Cathy Prendergast as she swings from the railings outside her house. She's got terrific black hair, the color of ink, that sways from side to side when she runs, and a freckly nose that burns in the sun. In bed at night I lie against the wall and commit mortal sins. Even though I am filled with shame, I cannot help myself. When I am grown-up and rich like her father we'll get married, Cathy and me.

Mam doesn't like The Prendergasts and she treats them with what my English teacher says is "condescension." When she gossips about Cathy's mother the Old Man tells her not to be so "bloody self-righteous."

Cathy is the prettiest girl in the world. Her brother, Mick has a glass eye and listens to Abba records all day long. Mam says he's a scut, and I should steer clear of him. We climb the apple tree in the Prendergast's back garden and sit in the tree house with glasses of Nash's red lemonade and bags of Tayto cheese 'n onion crisps. Cathy won't climb into the tree because she's afraid of tearing her dress. Tommy, Mick, and me throw apples at the cats in the lane. Sometimes we light cigarettes we've cadged from the older boys on the avenue, Mick plucks his glass eye out of the socket and plops it down on the palm of his hand.

There's a character in *Treasure Island* who has a stiff leg, and reminds me of our neighbor, John Carson, who can be recognized from a distance by his lopsided walk. His entire left leg is ramrod straight and he swings it around from back to front with each step. How he and his wife Nuala created two daughters perplexes Tommy and me, so we spend hours trying to figure out how the Carson's do "it." We use felt-tipped markers on pieces of scrap wallpaper to draw stick figure cartoons of the various ways we imagine them having it off, John's left leg disconnected on the floor.

Ciara, their daughter, tells us how their bedroom is in the rear downstairs room of the house. The room corresponds to our living room and it is strange that a married couple would sleep in a downstairs room when there are plenty of good-sized bedrooms upstairs.

We hatch a plan to find out the truth about John Carson's leg. It's Tommy's idea, of course, having been driven to the edges of boredom by his two adult sisters and their chatter about "diet" this, and "Slim Fast" that, all winter long. In truth, his sister, Martina, is as round as she is tall, a beach-ball shaped woman with heavy make-up and fiercely plucked eyebrows, with a voice as sharp as the edge of a butcher's knife. Her favorite phrase is, "A moment on your lips, a life-time on your hips."

We mock her roly-poly body and her obsession with Mills and Boon romance novels, with their nurses and teachers who go on exotic holidays and fall prey to foreign lovers with names like Raul and Pedro, only to be rescued by the hero, who is white, blond, and tall, with chiseled cheekbones.

On Wednesday when the moon is a sliver in the blue

night sky, we meet up at Tommy's garden gate. His house is three doors down from the Carson's yard, and we are going to sneak into the Carson's back garden. The plan is to try and see in through the curtains and catch John Carson having one-legged sex with his wife. In theory, the expedition should be a simple one: climb up onto their wall, drop down the other side, sneak through the bushes and sneak up to the window and get a look inside, then scarper.

When everyone is asleep I open my bedroom window and crawl out onto the roof of the garden shed. I drop onto Mam's rhododendron bushes and make my way to the garden gate. Once out in our back lane I creep along in the shadows, spy-like, turn onto the Rathgar Road, sidle along the outside of the first house on our road, along by the parked cars, until I reach the narrow lane that connects with the alley where Tommy's and the Carson's back doors are located.

I wait for five long minutes until Tommy finally shows. The wind moves the bushes, and some small mice or a predatory cat rustle in the undergrowth. This sets me on edge and I stick my hands deep in my pockets and breathe shallow, nervous breaths.

I bunt Tommy up the Carson's wall, because he's a good deal shorter than me, and then he reaches down and lends me a hand. We creep to the concrete area beneath the dining room window of the house. The windowsill is quite high, the square yard outside the kitchen and dining room sunk below the level of the garden.

"I can't see," he hisses. "Give me a bunt to the window ledge."

I knit my hands together and take his weight as his shoe rests in my hands. He pushes off and I totter a bit.

"He's got two legs!" he says. "He's got two legs!"

He drops to the ground and I wait to be lifted to the window to see the revelation. Tommy's grip is less secure than mine and I start to slide down the wall, but not before I manage to see through the opening in the curtains and there's John Carson in white Jockey briefs like the Old Man wears. His left leg is straight out in front of him and a long steel rod is attached by leather straps to his waist and ankle. His wife is on the bed with her nightdress open.

"Push me up again," I whisper. But Tommy can't hold me. Off the ledge of the window I tumble, and I try to catch the wall but fall instead onto Tommy and he topples against a steel dustbin. The lid clatters to the concrete.

"Shit! Run..." Tommy hisses.

The curtains open wide and light floods the yard. We sprint to the bushes. From there we watch the curtains close again and a few seconds later the back door opens. John Carson limps out into the yard and looks about. He sees the lid of the dustbin and picks it off the ground, careful to place it back on the cylindrical container with a bang. "Fecking cats," he mutters. His back to us, he drags his leg around and retreats.

We unlock the garden gate and go back out into the lane. We make the safety of the tree house where we fall on the floor breathing heavily, finally able to laugh at our narrow escape.

The moon and clouds paint the sky and I walk in shadows back to my own bedroom. In bed with my eyes closed I wonder what it must be like to have a leg that doesn't bend at all.

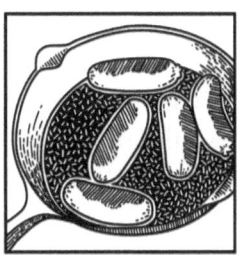

Chapter 2

The Old Man journeys home on the ferry from Stranraer, and catches the night train from Belfast, in time for breakfast. Mam grills Denny sausages and Galtee rashers to beat the band and has his breakfast on the table before he takes his pea coat off.

"Come here to me, son," he cries, and sweeps me into a bear hug. "Did you miss your Old Man? Did you?"

"I did. Yes," I reply. The smell of whiskey mixed with his Old Spice aftershave overpowers me. After righting me and giving my shoulder a squeeze, he dances me around the kitchen table and sings in his deep tenor, "For all that I found there I might as well be where the Mountains of Mourne sweep down to the sea."

I wriggle out of his grip, plunk myself down at my chair, and tip the cornflakes into the bowl, trying hard to ignore his good mood.

"Arrah, you'll dance with your ould fella, won't you, Helen?" he says to Mam, and drags her away from the cooker by the apron. Mam's face is crimson and her curly brown hair is askew, the cat's eye spectacles at an angle on her nose. The Old Man, grins double-chinned. He raises one bushy eyebrow and winks knowingly at me.

"Jesus, Ronan, I'll skull you if the sausages are burnt," she says.

"Give us a kiss, *mo chroí.*" He purses his lips and waits. Mam shakes her head and laughs, before she kisses him on his bumpy nose. His hand lands on her bottom and she yelps like the neighbor's Yorkshire terrier, but the look on her face is pure magic and she smiles more than she has in months.

He attempts to put an arm about her waist, but she's not having any of it. "Ah, go on. Won't I be back on the rig soon enough, and you'll be done with me once more?" he says.

"You're a disgrace," she says, and smooths her apron. She returns to the sizzling pan on the stove and he reaches for her waist and gives her one more twirl about the kitchen, his Brylcreemed hair immoveable, and his face flushed with excitement.

Their laughter fills the kitchen, mixes with the smell of the frying rashers and sausages, and we bask in this rare moment of good humor.

She sniffles into her cardigan sleeve and says, "Can't live with you, Ronan, and can't bloody well live without you."

The first day is all right, his bag stuffed with gifts from the Duty-Free. We have no idea what olive oil is and Mam dabs it behind her ears like perfume. By day two, I disappear into the wallpaper pattern. I'm deemed, "insufferable," and banished to my bedroom to play in silence.

By the end of the first week, Mam's patience is gone and she tells him, "You're my own peculiar crown of thorns, you are."

She complains bitterly to her friends who come over for morning cups of tea, how the Old Man is "no better than a baby who needs constant attention, and won't raise a finger to help around the house." Their arguments lead the Old Man to abandon the ship of home for the safe harbor of the local snug. I don't know what to do now except keep out of his way.

I jump up and down on the brassy bed and pretend I'm Eric Clapton. The mattress creaks and the lights below in the sitting room sway to and fro as the Old Man tries to nap.

He roars, "I'm not at sea anymore," and "Stop your nonsense, or I'll put a stop to it for you."

I hurry down to the sitting room and ask if he'll play soccer with me.

"Don't annoy me," he says.

"But, Da, you said you'd come to the park and play football with me," I say.

He shifts in his chair and blows his nose. "Not now, not now. I'm only home five minutes. Give a man a bit of time to recover, will you? I'll play with you soon enough," he says.

I know he won't though. He's always too tired. Before he lost the business, he'd bring me to the park and kick the ball as high in the air as he could. Once he hit a crow and it fell unconscious to the ground, and when I suggested we take it to a vet he laughed at me.

Mam says, "Go out and play in God's good fresh air, or I'll give you a lick of the wooden spoon for your trouble. Your father and I have to do the bills. You'll walk to the park with him when we're done."

We often take a walk in Bushy Park, usually down by the duck pond where petrified birds sit cold-arsed in the water.

All the Old Man does with me is walk to the park and complain about the family business getting taken away by the banks. I wish he'd spend time with me the way Tommy does with his father; fishing for tadpoles or watching Buster Crabbe matinees at the Kenilworth Cinema. The Old Man hates the cinema and says the dark makes him unhappy.

Tommy and his father built a model railway set-up with

mountains and tunnels in their back shed. I don't know why we can't build a racetrack for my toy cars, or why he doesn't teach me to play chess. Anything would be better than what he does, but he is my Dad, and that's what matters most.

"He has his reasons," Mam says, and even though I know that's right, it doesn't make the pain in my chest go away. In a way, he's a bit like Jesus; I'm supposed to love him unconditionally and not question anything he says.

I ask if there are any fish in the pond, and he says a man he knows once caught a whopper with a silver spinner and a bit of twine. I dig in the mud with a stick, in search of treasures, and find a deep-green bottle with a cork in it. He says Mam will know if it's an old medicine bottle or not, because her father was a chemist in the country.

She is delighted when I show it to her, and, as she clinks the glass with a fork, says, "It's the same as the ones my father filled with prescriptions."

Her eyes fill with tears and I give her a hug. I can tell she's sad. I never met her father because he died after World War II of a heart attack. "He came over all funny," she says. "A good-looking man he was, like a movie star."

Am I more like my Mam's father than I am my Old Man's side of the family? To check, I sneak up to Granny's room at the back of the house, sliding my slippers along the carpet. The room smells of old person, and Granny's hair net is on the dressing table; the grey hairs trapped in it are like some dead creature's skin. In the lamplight, I look at the framed photograph of my grandfather on the wall. He is not handsome, and has the same ugly ears that I do.

Granny has more tests in the hospital and won't be home for a few days. Mam is worried and cries at the ironing board in the kitchen. The Old Man is off back to Scotland on Monday and Mam is busy ironing his clothes and making sure all the loose buttons are stitched properly onto his pea coat so they don't end up falling into the North Sea. She sniffs back a tear when she thinks I'm not looking. The Old Man has disappeared for one last pint at the pub and will likely come home at dinnertime, polluted.

The Old Man announces out of the blue that we're going to watch a soccer match. On Sunday morning when he gets home from Mass he's got a proud look on his face and he withdraws two narrow tickets from his breast pocket. "Shamrock Rovers are playing Bohemians at Glenmalure Park. I had to beg for these tickets."

Mam mutters something about "Rushing the Sunday lunch," but I know she'll spend the time we're away at the match in peace, smoking cigarette after cigarette in the back garden. Even the organized beds of roses and dianthus have lost their fragrance, and reek of smoke.

I'm beside myself with excitement. I've never been to a professional soccer match before, and even though "The Searchers," is on television and I love how John Wayne rides his horse into the river and plucks the girl out of the water without stopping, I can't wait to walk to Milltown and watch Shamrock Rovers with the Old Man.

Mam has Sunday lunch on the table at one o'clock and the Old Man attacks the Minestrone soup and ham sandwiches with vigor. His slurping annoys Mam and she sits silently in her chair waiting for him to stop.

While she clears the dishes, the Old Man buttons his mackintosh and wraps a scarf about his neck. "We'd better be heading off," he says, handing me my anorak, the one with the Eskimo-fur collar.

Throngs of people are walking along the Milltown Road towards the football ground. A high wall topped with barbed wire surrounds it. Through the turnstiles we go, the gate clicking as it rotates. Inside the terraces are filled with groups of supporters wearing green-and-white-hooped jerseys, and in the far corner a smaller group are in black-and-red-striped jerseys—the Bohemians' fans.

"Those gurriers are the enemy," the Old Man says.

The crowd chants, "In your Drumcondra slums, you look in the dustbin for something to eat, you find a dead rat and you think it's a treat, in your Drumcondra slums."

I burrow my head into my anorak and try to disappear. I've never heard anything like it before. The crowd roars, "You're going to get your fucking heads kicked in."

The small group of Bohemians' fans chant, "Bo-hezz! Bo-hezz," and wave their scarves over their heads. As the teams run out the place goes mad. Under the corrugated iron shed the ground we're standing on shakes as the crowd jumps up and down in anticipation. When the whistle blows there's silence, then the roar, "Come on you Gree-yins."

The truth is plain; both teams are rotten compared to watching Liverpool on the telly.

At half-time we shuffle to a small concrete hut at the back of the stands and the Old Man forks over a £10 note and says to the wrinkled woman in the nylon blue coat, "give us two steak-and-kidney pies and cups of Bovril, love."

We stand against the rail sipping the beefy water and a man wearing a deerstalker hat strides along the sideline towards the corner flag. The crowd sings, "Sherlock, Sherlock give us a wave," and don't let up. At the corner flag, he picks at the grass and flings a clod to the side. The crowd gets louder and the man touches the brim of his hat. "SHERLOCK!!!"

"Soak it in, Son. This is a grand day out," the Old Man says, clapping his hands together.

"Yes, Da." I unbutton the horn-shaped buttons on my anorak and rework them crookedly for fun. My feet hurt from standing on the cold concrete. "Band on the Run," plays on the loudspeakers and the Old Man goes on about, "hippies and jungle music," his mouth full of steak-and-kidney pie.

The teams trot out again and the trill of the referee's

whistle rents the air. The man beside us bellows, "Come on you fookin' Gree-yins!"

A duck flaps across the cloudy sky and I count its wing-beats as it disappears in the distance. I don't know what caused the Old Man to bring me to the match, but it's the first time I can remember us doing something together where neither of us ended up angry with the other.

Mam brings a plate of scones and mugs of tea for us when we return from the game. That night we sit in front of the black and white television and watch the Riordan's on RTE. The Old Man loves the rural scuttlebutt and roars with laughter when Batty Brennan gets an earful from his wife, Minnie. I'm happier turning the pages of Mark Twain and finding out what happens inside Injun Joe's cave, but we've bonded over the soccer match and for the first time in my life I know what it's like to have a dad who does things with you.

The Old Man has a coughing fit and he's blue-faced and Mam thumps him on the back. He falls back into his chair, his jowls berry-colored, and his eyes bloodshot.

"You'll kill me yet," he tells Mam, crumpling the pages of the newspaper and crossing his legs in front of him.

I cringe on the floor as they argue. The door slams and Mam storms off to the kitchen. The walls of the house shake and his anger floats fast to the top of the house where it gets trapped and echoes forever.

In the kitchen Mam is trembling. I run upstairs to get away from the yelling. His anger is the color of bruises—the color of winter skies. When the house quiets as he heads out to the pub I venture downstairs.

Mam is outside at this point, puffing on a cigarette, toeing the swath of weeds that are choking her carnations. I know she's angry because her arms are crossed and she keeps trying to ignite the lighter in the driving wind. The bed sheets billow on the clothesline, trapped clouds trying to escape the ground.

A tender look from her brings me close to tears and I look away at the house sparrows on the roof, small and distant.

"He has me exhausted," she says, blowing a ring of smoke into the air.

"Sorry," I say, as I fiddle with the laces of my boots. "You saved his life. Why is he so angry?"

"Ah, Son. He's doing the best he can." She wipes the corner of her eye, takes the cigarette lighter and puts the flame to another cigarette. "He doesn't mean the things he says. You know he loves us very much," she says.

We have a roast beef for dinner, and I'm sure beef must be almost extinct, the amount of it we eat. The Old Man sops the bit of blood in the middle with a bit of Yorkshire pudding, though I prefer pork with applesauce and roast potatoes.

I love pork crackling and how it crunches between my teeth. Granny sits with us and pokes her food around the plate, but she doesn't eat much at all. She wears lipstick and rouge and looks strange, like an Aunt Sally doll. Mam smiles at her and pats her hand now and then.

If she gets worse, Mam says, they might send her to the lunatic asylum. I don't want Granny to end up there, because I don't want to have to visit her in a cell with lots of other lunatics.

Mam takes her back upstairs when dinner is over and for a change the Old Man and I do the dishes; or rather, I do them. He says Mam's at the end of her tether, and this means she's ready to start another row with him if he doesn't mind his manners.

It pelts down rain the next morning so I wear my wool duffel coat with the artificial horn fasteners and heavy hooded collar to school. The coat soaks up the rain like a sponge.

I give the Old Man a hug goodbye. He smells of beer and Old Spice, and his eyes are bloodshot. "Be a good *gossoon* for your mother. She needs your help around the house while I'm away. Take out the bins each week. Do your homework. Stay out of trouble. I'll bring you back a Toblerone if you're a good man."

The Old Man his hand through my hair at the front door and taps the barometer to see what the weather is going to do. He waves me off from the door, his arm around Mam's shoulders. Usually, I cycle to school, but it's raining so hard I decide to take the bus from the Terenure Road, get off at the bottom of Templeville Road and hustle to school in a throng of classmates.

Banjo Anderson, our math teacher, plays us "Bennie and the Jets" on his portable record player. He wears a bright yellow sports coat and has hair down to his shoulders that the other teachers talk about in hushed voices.

In the parking lot when I got my bike from the racks the other day, Father McDaid said he was "A bloody hippie. And an egomaniac. He's bloody soporific, with all that New Age teaching nonsense he spouts." He was still at it when I pedaled off in a spray of pebbles. I didn't want to hear him say anything else bad about Banjo, so I stood out of the saddle and pedaled at full speed down Templeville Road.

I'm in class, daydreaming about Cathy Prendergast, so I slip my hand into my pants because of the itch. Banjo yaks on about Pythagoras and I try to make sure I'm not spotted by any of my classmates. My eyes closed, I'm afraid to look in case Banjo spots me and drags me to the front of the class. But I feel damp, sticky and nasty.

"Teacher, teacher!" Mick Lambert says.

"What is it, Lambert? Can't you see that Pythagorean geometry is important?"

"Brogan there's after giving himself an organism," he says, and points straight at me. I'm scarlet, wriggle in my chair, and try to look innocent.

"Get up here, you filthy beast," Banjo says, as he takes a

step towards me.

He makes me stand at the top of the class motionless. The boys laugh and point at my trousers.

"He's wet his pants!" someone yells out.

"Silence." Banjo slams his hand on the table.

I jump and he cuffs me on the ear. "Get out. You better go home and change. Take a bath, or something. I'll see you in the Headmaster's office after lunch." He pushes me to the door, and I grab my schoolbag and make a run for the bike racks.

I try to sneak in the door, but Mam hears my key in the latch and is out of the kitchen. "Why are you home from school for the love of God? I'm about to make brown bread for your tea."

"Mam, you might get a phone call from Mr. Anderson."

"What did you do? Out with it," she says, and wipes her floury hands on the apron.

I tell her some watered-down version of what happened and she shakes her head and points up the stairs. "I'll handle this, because if your father hears about it you're off to Borstal."

I strip down in the bathroom and run the hot water and the tears come freely. A splatter of mud on my face makes it look as if I've a beauty spot, but it is dirt. The soap is in the mermaid-shaped holder, next to the candle the Old Man lights when he has to do his business.

Mam continues to read me the riot act, and tells me all about how it's a mortal sin to do what I did. She writes the details in the ledger for the Old Man to review.

"You'll grow warts on your hands if you ever do that again," she says, shoving me out the door to go back to school. I swing my leg over the crossbar and make the lonely trek back to face the music, and a magpie stares at me from the railings.

Father Tubridy, the headmaster, and Banjo usher me into the office where I hold my hand out and wait for the swish of the leather strap. Before it descends, I withdraw my hand and it misses.

"Stay still and take your punishment like a man."

He grips my hand with his free one and gives me three good lashes. My whole arm tingles and my eyes are full of tears.

"Good Man, now. Get back to class and behave yourself appropriately. And you can expect five decades of the Holy Rosary when you go to confession."

Chapter 3

The bells ring out from the Church of the Three Patrons for ten o'clock Sunday Mass, and Saints Patrick, Bridget, and Columba, statued above the portico, huddle together for warmth. Outside, neighbors golosh their way towards the church, and pass beneath my bedroom window in winter coats bedecked with gilt brooches, over-applied perfume and toilet water, kidskin gloves and fur stoles. I can usually tell who's who from the footfalls, but the crunch of frost smothers their footsteps and I struggle out of bed and into my cold clothes, to peek out the window to identify the passers-by.

Wool-gloved, ears red and pained from the cold, the Old Man and I make our way through the gray streets, cars decorated with slush, as crows and house sparrows jostle for a place on the telephone wires. By the old Taoiseach's house, the crackle of a transistor radio comes from the small security hut inside the front gate. Two blue-uniformed Gardaí are outside, cigarettes cupped in hands, and their walkie-talkies crackle away. Slushed snow crunches underfoot as I go by, head down, no eye contact. At the intersection of Garville Avenue and the Rathgar Road, Cathy Prendergast walks along with her mother, who is a more mature, gorgeous version of Cathy. When they cross the road, I follow them, the hem of her mother's coat soaked by the wet snow. Cathy glances over her shoulder and I avert my eyes in case I might turn to stone. She winks at me and the tips of my ears burn.

White-and-red-cassocked altar boys surround Father McDaid as he spreads his arms wide at the altar, intoning, "In the name of the Father, the Son, and the Holy Ghost."

All the while Cathy is in my sights. On my way back from communion, she coughs, and as I try to dislodge the host from the roof of my mouth, I imagine her under the sycamore trees by the canal, my lips on hers.

We stop to speak to the new parish priest after Mass. According to Father O'Byrne, recently arrived from Youghal, the home of fine carpets, "The path of the righteous man is beset on all sides by the inequities of the selfish, and the tyranny of evil men."

The Old Man nods when he hears these words. He sucks in his stomach and draws himself to his full height as he shakes the new priest's hand. He winces as the Old Man's grip tightens.

"Grand sermon, Father. This young fellow will do well to stop his skiving and say more prayers. You wouldn't believe what sort of filthy behavior he was carrying on with at school last month," he says.

"Oh, I'm sure he's a righteous young soldier of Christ," the priest says.

"He's nothing of the sort," the Old Man says. "I gave him a harsh reminder of the path he should be focused on, and make no mistake about it."

He did, too. My hands stung for days and every time the coal scuttle needed to be filled I had to shovel it full, despite the blisters on my hands.

"Spare the rod, spare the rod," the priest says. Adding, "Good day to you, now."

"And the same to you, Father," the Old Man says, as he pushes me along towards the church gates.

The next day after tea we drive over to the Dundrum Shopping Center to buy our Christmas tree. It's tradition to put it up by the 6th of December, but Mam wanted to wait until the Old Man was home before we got ours. As we drive past the enormous gates of the Central Mental Asylum I try to picture the lunatics inside wearing their straitjackets and drooling at the mouth. The Old Man sometimes says, "There but for the grace of God goes me!"

Mam adds, "Aren't we already living in Cloud-cuckoo-land?"

The place we get our tree from is in a corner of the parking lot and the trees lean against a chain-link fence like toppled soldiers. The Old Man wants the biggest one we can manage, but Mam walks the ranks and picks out one a bit taller than her. She says the tree is a Nobilis and is sufficient for our needs.

The man who sells the trees suggests we get that kind because it sheds fewer needles. He's awfully helpful and gives the Old Man a hand as he fastens it to the top of the car. After we're done we drive it home in the sleet. The Old Man declares it, "foul weather," and the windscreen wipers bang rhythmically as we navigate the wet city streets.

We drag the boxes of decorations from under the stairs where they've lived since the previous Christmas. We think the triangular space is the pantry, but Aunt Martha has a real pantry, with windows and a glass door. Hers is stuffed. Ours is the place where things go to die. On a shelf at the back of our pantry cardboard boxes gather, filled with old clothes that no longer fit, and albums of ancient black-and-white snapshots of dead relatives and friends.

Fairy lights uncoil on the carpet like the skeleton of an

ancient reptile. Painted glass balls frosted with sparkles sit in tissue paper, some of them shattered into small pieces, some spared. Other decorations attach to the tree limbs with pipe cleaners, elves perch precariously above the steel bucket that holds the trunk in place. The Old Man fills the bucket with soil from the flowerbed in the back garden and sets the tree inside it. He believes in shortcuts and prefers to prop up the tree in the corner, which he says cuts out the need for any kind of elaborate anchoring system.

Mam shakes her head and covers the bucket with last year's wrapping paper, making sure to put the ripped bits at the back. This method works well for the most part, mainly because our white cat, the one who scaled the tree after an elf the previous year, is now buried in the shadow of the garden shed. This year, there's no need to police the house to ensure the cat doesn't topple the tree. Mam is too proper to say she's glad the cat had died, but I know she hated the beast. She is from the country and has strong views on issues like pets and pasteurization, and believes animals need to be useful.

The Old Man ties the tip of the expertly-trimmed tree to the rail that runs around the top of the room, and declares it to be "game ball."

Mam unfurls the paper-chains and I steady the chair as she attaches them to the chandelier in the center of the room. When she stretches them into the corners, the room brightens. On the mantelpiece, she places a sprig of holly with shiny red berries in each of the Waterford crystal vases. "Even though we've suffered some reversals in our fortunes, we still do it up for the holidays," she says.

By Christmas Eve, the space beneath the tree overflows with her expertly wrapped packages, because the Old Man is no good at that kind of thing, and he's already into the Jameson's like a baby with a bottle. This year I want a guitar, so I can be like Eric Clapton in Cream, and at night when I say my prayers I ask God for it. I know that this won't happen because I heard them fight about the Old Man's pay packet. Whenever he comes home from the North Sea and hands the brown envelope to Mam she shakes her head and asks how he manages to spend so much of his wages when he's trapped on an oilrig for the entire time. She sorts the notes into a pile and hands a few back to him so he can walk up the road for a pint later.

Granny is in the armchair by the fire, another of her Mills and Boon Romance books open on her lap, and I'm by the fire with my Topper comic. The lights from the tree twinkle, and the room is Ali Baba's treasure cave. The Old Man reads the horse racing reports for Saturday's races in Fairyhouse, and Mam punches holes in a pattern sheet for her electric knitting machine.

The Old Man wants to drive down to Kinnegad to collect the turkey for the Christmas dinner from our old butcher's shop. Mam says I can go with him if I bundle up and stay inside the car. She would come with us, but she can't leave Granny alone in the house since she was found in the village shops in her nightgown the other day.

I fiddle with the lint in my pocket and the Old Man says, "Get into the car and stop your fiddling about."

"Now be sure to arrive at Eamon's by three. He'll be off for the Christmas himself," Mam says.

The Old Man hums Christmas Carols and taps the steering wheel with his fingers, and I wish I could be getting ready for an expedition to the North Pole instead of listening to him butcher, "Adeste Fideles."

By green fields with black-and-white cows we go, and finally pull up in front of Eamon's shop, the blinds down, lights off. "Scutter. The fecker is gone," the Old Man says. "Look, stay here while I go into Jack's Roadhouse to see a man about a bird." He can barely control the laughter and almost chokes before disappears into the pub next-door.

I kick at the back of his seat once he's out of sight. I can't believe how much he drinks in a day, and God knows what he drinks when he's away on the oilrigs. I know Mam will have a conniption when she discovers we've no turkey for the Christmas dinner and I dread the fight that's going to ruin our holiday.

The Old Man wanders back smelling more of Guinness and whiskey than before. "We're in luck. I got the nod about an old lad getting rid of his last few birds." We drive up some narrow lanes filled with puddles, before we come to a halt at a farmhouse with a rusted green barn. The Old Man gets out and approaches a farmer who stands by the door of a thatched cottage.

"Soft day, thank God," the farmer says.

"It is indeed. Listen, a chap in Jack's Roadhouse said you might have a turkey to sell me. The butcher is gone for the day and the wife expects me home with a bird for the dinner."

"Oh, by the hokey, I have the perfect thing. Come around the back of the barn and I'll fix you right up," the farmer says.

A small wire pen rests against the barn wall. "There she is, God Bless her," the farmer says. He points at a haggard bird. "Five quid and she's all yours."

"But, she's alive. I need her plucked and the giblets removed," the Old Man says.

"And I want to win the Sweepstakes," the farmer says. "Take it or leave it."

The Old Man peels a note from his wallet and hands it to the farmer.

"Are you certain that bird is a turkey?" the Old Man asks. "Isn't it a bit on the small side?"

"Arrah, it's the runt of the litter. Hold on now and I'll stun her," the farmer says. He grabs hold of a shovel, swipes the turkey on the head, and lets it fall to the ground. He ties the bird up with twine and sticks it in a burlap sack marked, "Red

Mills Poultry Feed," and thrusts it into the Old Man's waiting arms.

Once the bird is shut in the trunk of the car, we drive back to the city in silence. We pull up in front of the house and he says, "Let me handle your mother. I'll leave the turkey in the boot for a bit yet."

The house is full of the scent of plum pudding when we walk in, and Mam is boiling white Tupperware bowls on the stove in the big saucepans.

The Old Man's is empty handed, and Mam asks, "Where's the bird?"

"Ah, it's a long story. I have it in the trunk all ready to go," he says.

"Well, bring it in, then. Bring it in. I'd better get it dressed and stuffed for tomorrow."

He returns with the sack, and a strange low wail leaks out.

"Are you doolally?" Mam asks. "It's alive."

"Well, to be honest, Eamon's was shut when we got there, so I found a fellow out the Galway Road..."

"Ah, you stopped for a drink, didn't you? Tell the truth, now?"

"We had to go into the Salmon Leap Inn to make our business. Didn't we, Son?" the Old Man says, with a wink.

"Yes, Mam. Da had to go to the toilet. We didn't stay long," I reply. I know I'm caught in a lie and that it's wrong and I wish the Old Man wouldn't make me lie for him.

"Oh, you have the boy telling fibs, now. God forgive you," Mam says, swatting him with the dishcloth. "Show me the damned bird."

He unties the string and a red, wattled head pokes out and pecks at his fingers.

"Fecking beast bit me," he cries, and drops the sack on the floor.

The bird wriggles out and flaps about the kitchen. It stumbles into chairs, feathers fly and the thump of it as it bumps into the stove and then the fridge frightens the wits out of it.

"Do you know what?" Mam says to the Old Man, "You're a fecking eejit. That's no more turkey than I am. You were sold a bloody chicken."

She pushes past the Old Man and says, "Come here, you beauty," making a grab for its neck. She wraps her arms about the bird and holds it tight to her chest. "Open the back door," she orders, and as I undo the bolt and push the door wide she lets the bird loose in the yard. "Go on, Ronan, get out there and finish that poor unfortunate creature off with the coal shovel."

The Old Man goes into the yard and Mam slams the door behind him. A minute later there's a horrible squeal from the yard and the Old Man returns triumphant with the corpse limp in his hands.

Mam takes the fowl from him, wipes her hands and snorts. "You're good for bloody nothing," she tells him.

The Old Man wipes his nose with his hanky and says, "I'm off to the pub for a quick one." He takes his hat and leaves Mam and me in a room surrounded by plum puddings and dead chickens, the letterbox rattling in his wake.

When she calms down she says, "Go up and check on your grandmother. Make sure she's got the hot water bottle at her feet." Mam places the dead bird in a pot of salted water and puts it to the boil so she can de-feather it.

Granny is asleep, her knit cap on her head and her false teeth in the water glass on the bedside table. She looks like one of the dead crusaders in the crypt of St. Michan's church that I saw on a school outing, and even shook hands with too. I close the door softly and disappear down to the sitting room with my book.

Mam is in a stew on Christmas morning because of the

turkey and the Old Man's shenanigans. She stirs the porridge as the Old Man reads the paper. She bangs the dish down in front of him without a word and he barely looks up from the obituaries. I hate when they slam doors and don't speak, and then when they make up the Old Man swears he'll never lose his temper again. I know he lies because his eyelid twitches, and because mine does the same when I lie. The smell of their anger blends into the scent of the Christmas tree, ornaments attached—painted shells of Nativity scene and frosted snowmen.

The dinner table is set with the best linen and silver candlesticks. Tureens of Cumberland and bread sauces wait for the turkey and ham, and gilt-decorated Christmas crackers are at each of our plates. Mam already has the smoked salmon with brown bread and home-made mayonnaise at our places, too.

The Old Man smacks his lips and forks slice after slice of the ham and turkey onto his plate. Brussel sprouts and roast potatoes steam in their dishes and we eat in silence, save the loud ticks of the carriage clock on the mantelpiece.

He turns the lights off and Mam pours the brandy on the plum pudding and ignites it with one of the tall candles on the table. We clap as the flames crisp the dessert and she brings the brandy butter and whipped cream from the kitchen.

By the time dinner is over we've listened to the Pope's message to the world and both Mam and the Old Man are half-drunk on red wine. The Old Man slouches in the chair, and a black and white film lulls him to sleep. The tinny speaker pours out, "There'll be bluebirds over the white cliffs of Dover." Gracie Fields gives me a sympathetic smile and turns to her uniformed lover for a kiss.

"This is the best day of the year," I say, books and presents piled by the armchair where Mam is busy doing the Irish Times' Christmas Crossword. My favorite present is an Alice in Wonderland-themed chess set. I don't really know how to play, but our neighbor, Mr. O'Malley is going to give me lessons.

The fire goes out and the National Anthem comes on the TV, Mam says it's time for all good soldiers to go to bed, so I kiss her good night and do the same to the Old Man who is fast asleep in his chair, his left leg twitching, and the false teeth hanging crookedly from his mouth.

Chapter 4

I'm taking chess lessons, and because the Old Man doesn't know how to play, Daddy O'Malley will teach me in the afternoons a few times a week. Today is my first lesson and I'm learning all about how the pieces move.

"One two, there or there," Daddy O'Malley directs as he slides the black plastic horse in an L-shaped direction on the chessboard, his voice as soft as soft can be; the low drawl of the Derry accent telling me how to move the horse.

"Time for tea me little man," he says after a while, rising to go put the kettle on. I grasp the white horse and move it in the same L-shaped way he maneuvered the black one on the board a moment ago. I'm getting the hang of it, after going through pawns, rooks and now knights.

Silver-haired and stooped, Daddy O'Malley hasn't worked in the four years he's lived next door. Himself and the Old Man struck up an instant friendship because he knows what it's like to leave his hometown and put down roots somewhere else. He often spends hours telling stories of the "struggle." The Old Man isn't a particularly fervent nationalist but he loves to listen to stories of IRA campaigns and he doesn't agree with the modern IRA at all. He deems them "Thugs," and says they're only interested in violence for violence's sake.

Daddy O'Malley smokes like a chimney, lighting cigarette after cigarette, the pile of butts in the ashtray making a little mountain. When the faucet whooshes hot water, Daddy O'Malley puts down his cigarette and puts the kettle on the hob. I grab his cigarette butt and suck in hard. The hot smoke catches in my throat and I cough stale air, trying to catch my breath.

"Lord God, what in the world are you doing there," he asks, turning around and catching me in the act.

"I... I… wanted to be like you."

He tweaks my nose with thumb and forefinger, pretending to have removed its tip. "You'll have to practice then," he says. "But, you can no tell your folks."

I nod and he lights a Dunhill cigarette, the green box flat and square on the table.

"Watch," he says, and sucks in gently, holding his breath. He expels the smoke through his nostrils in a steady stream. He looks like an out-of-fire dragon.

"Here, you try now, little man."

I take the cigarette and mimic what I've seen. The breath explodes from my mouth. My eyes leak tears and my stomach feels odd. I don't like this smoking thing but I want to act grown up. I promise to try and do better next time.

When it gets dark and Mam is asleep by the fire, I sneak into the kitchen and open her handbag. It smells of cigarettes and *Eau De Cologne 1711*. The blue bottle rests in the bottom of the handbag. On top of it, a pack of burgundy and gold cigarettes: Thomas Dunhill & Sons. I open the packet and pull out two of the long white sticks. Slipping them into my trouser pocket, I head upstairs to the jakes. I bolt the door and open the small square window. It's a few feet above the toilet bowl and looks out on the O'Malley's yard.

The redheaded match flashes on the strip and I put the flame to the cigarette. I inhale, imitating Daddy O'Malley. It's the same way Mam smokes hers.

I exhale out the window with my feet balanced precariously on the edge of the bath. Twenty minutes and two cigarettes later I unlock the door and unsteadily slip down the stairs and into the living room to watch *Blue Peter* on the BBC, with Mam fast asleep in the Old Man's armchair. The Old Man is still away at the pub and God knows what time of day or night he'll reappear.

Mam wakes and goes out to turn the radiator on in her bedroom. I'm in front of the fire when she shouts out.

"Patrick? Get out here," Mam's voice carries from the upstairs landing.

I walk up the stairs to where she stands, arms folded, at the door to the jakes. She wrinkles her nose, eyebrows arching simultaneously, and takes a deep breath. "Do you think I came down in the last shower?"

I don't know what you mean, Mam," I say, crossing my fingers behind my back. The smell of cigarettes is faint, but she has a nose for trouble and I can sense the wooden spoon is not far away.

"Were you smoking in here?' She asks.

"Uh, no."

"Well, you must take me for a right eejit then. I can smell the bloody smoke. Was it the ghosts again?"

"Sorry. I was practicing what I learned in O'Malley's."

"What? Jesus, Mary, and Joseph. Did that old simpleton have you smoking? I thought you were there for chess lessons."

"I took the butt. He tried to stop me but then he showed me how to do it. The way you do too."

"Oh, 'clare to the Lord," she sighs. "I'll bloody well wring his neck."

I feel bad for Daddy O'Malley, and worse for myself when Mam records my behavior in the ledger for the Old Man to see when he gets home from the pub tonight.

I promise to not smoke ever again after the Old Man administers the punishment for my crime. I also tell the priest in the confession box about it, and he lands me with a penance of six Our Fathers and fifteen Hail Marys. For the rest of the Christmas Holidays I try not to be a burden, and find ways to help Mam cope with all that's on her plate.

Granny is in hospital for some tests because she has a strange bump on her nose. I gathered up the bedclothes from her room so they can be cleaned and aired before she gets back. I know this means a little less work for Mam, and she might be a little happier because of my help.

Mam visited Granny this morning and when she got home, the Old Man said we should go for a spin to take her mind off her mother, so we take a run up to the Sally Gap, close to Mullaghcleevaun Mountain.

Our car is an Austin Wolseley with the back seats missing because the Old Man used them for a makeshift sofa in the sitting room before we could afford a proper one. He couldn't manage to put the seat back properly, so now it's stored in the garden shed collecting cobwebs. The springs and coils extend from the floor and dangle in mid-air. I get to sit on an old couch cushion Daddy O'Malley gave us when he got a new sofa.

We wait in the car outside the Coach House bar while the Old Man goes inside to "wet his whistle," a maneuver that involves urinating, drinking a glass of Jameson's and a pint of Guinness. Mam sits in the front seat puffing away on a cigarette, muttering about oilrigs and Acts of God. He gets back in the car and raises an arse-cheek, cracks a fart and blames it on, "The bubbles in the blackstuff."

"Jesus, Mary and Joseph, I should have listened to my mother when she told me not to marry you. She said you had a low streak in you," Mam says.

As we ascend into the pine woods, I try to make myself invisible, caught between the broken springs and poisonous fumes. The Old Man declares there to be "no greater sight in Christendom, and adds, "Sure, why would a soul ever want to holiday abroad?"

Mam lights another cigarette and seethes in a cloud, her fear of heights triggered by the sheer drop at the side of the road, made worse by the Old Man's unsteady driving.

"Mind what you're doing," she screams, as the Old Man jars the wheel to take us closer to the edge. "You're in no condition to drive these roads," she adds, and demands he stop the car until the drink subsides.

He knows his limits and pulls to the verge, where he tucks his chin on his chest and takes a nap. Wild birds wheel and caw in the wind. The windows steam up and I play *Xs* and *Os* with my finger, drawing the grid and marking dots in the condensation.

When he finally wakes, he pontificates some more about the glory of the Irish countryside and how it's always good to get out of the city and breathe God's good air into our lungs.

Mam's clicking needles mark time until we reach our destination. The winding roads make my stomach feel bad and I sit in the back seat—book open, the corners eaten away, line drawings well-thumbed—trying to take my mind off the journey.

We finally stop at the Meeting of the Waters in Avoca, where there's a seat created by the roots of a tree, under which the poet Sir Thomas Moore composed his poems. Mam spreads the blanket on the ground, opens the Tupperware containers of salad and sandwiches for our tea. The Old Man wanders off to one of the trees and the next thing she berates him for piddling on Thomas Moore's tree.

"Go away out of that. It's not a sin. A bit of widdle never hurt a living thing," he says, with a wink.

Mam rattles the salad with her fork, the tips of her ears reddening the way they do before a fight. I look away at the limbs of another tree and the shadows striping the ground. It seems the sort of tree you could tie a person to, blindfold them, and then execute them for treason, pulling the trigger slowly to make them wet their pants before dying.

"Eat your sandwiches," she says, distracting me from my daydreams. I sniff the egg and mayonnaise mixture and make a face. The car will be even more of a gas factory on the way home.

Returning from Avoca we detour to the round tower at Glendalough. It stands straight up in the sky like a rocket ship. We have a photo of it on the kitchen dresser, but in real life it's even more fantastic. Mam tells me all about it while the Old Man mooches about at the edge of a stream looking for fish. I run to him and decide to hop across the water on some mossy rocks.

"Mind yourself," Mam says.

I'm the middle of the stream, when my foot slips on a moss-covered rock. Next thing, the world is frozen in time and the clouds stop in mid-air. I gasp for breath and swallow the freezing cold river water. My head goes dizzy and the Old Man pulls me from the water and pushes on my stomach. Half-digested egg sandwiches spray out of my mouth as he curses.

"Stop yelling at the lad," Mam says, putting her hand on his arm. He shrugs it off and keeps up his antics.

"The boy needs to wake his ideas up and stop acting the bloody maggot."

The Old Man finally stops shouting. Mam shakes her head. "You know, your father isn't angry at you; he's afraid after what happened," she says. "It's the way he shows his love for you, God help him." Afraid and sad: I realize this is the only way he can express his love. Unlike the other dads I know who play with and talk to their children, he "does" things, like saving my life, and putting food on the table for the family so we won't starve.

I've never looked closely at why he treats me this way. What Mam says makes plenty of sense considering how upset he gets at me, and then how he calms down and tries to apologize for hurting my feelings. But the damage is done.

Mam folds the tablecloth and I help her put the cutlery inside the Tupperware, while the Old Man sounds off about the sacrifices he's made for the family by working on the oil-rigs. She snorts, bundles our things into the boot of the car and lights a cigarette for the journey home.

Wrapped in the picnic blanket, a Famous Five book open on my lap, the clacks of Mam's knitting needles fill the car. Soon enough, the lights of the city are a faint glow to the East.

Chapter 5

The Old Man shows up with a dozen early snowdrops wrapped in newspaper on Mam's birthday; which she later discovers to be stolen from Mrs. Rooney's garden. She makes a clicking noise with her tongue, as if to say, "I know you didn't buy these yourself." The stew bubbles on the cooker and Mam digs in the pantry for a suitable vase to display the pilfered blooms.

He has also produced a birthday card. This is the first year he's remembered her birthday on time. He usually turns up with something a few days late after she's sulked and stewed over his forgetfulness. She laughs because he's misspelled her name, but I can tell it is not a good laugh from the way her lower lip sticks out over the upper one. Luckily, it's dinnertime and she's busy setting the table. I say nothing about the card, or the snowdrops.

I'm reminded of the American TV shows where they say things like, "Did you get that memo?" or "Do you catch my drift?" The Old Man missed the memo on Mam's birthday,

I'm certain. I know if I do say anything Mam will give me a clip of the wooden spoon.

The announcer on RTE1 Radio News says there's to be a ceasefire in the North of Ireland between the IRA and the British army. The Old Man shakes his head and spoons more stew into his mouth. Thirty-three chews per mouthful. According to Uncle Harry that's the key to proper digestion. Because I'm so focused on the chewing I don't speak for the entire meal. The Old Man goes on and on about the political unrest in the North of Ireland and blames the "Prods" for everything. I work my mouth around a large bit of gristle and burn my lip on the hot potato.

He says, "Steady as she goes. Steady as she goes."

I eat faster so I can go to my bedroom and read in peace, but he slams a fist on the table, making me jump.

"Why don't you teach this young gurrier manners," he says to Mam.

I scurry to the kitchen and light the candles on her cake before he starts World War III. When I bring the cake to the table we sing to her, and after she blows out the candles a sort of peace descends.

Mam loves the book of Irish verse I got for her at Greene's bookshop next to Trinity College, and recites some lines from Yeats's, "The Circus Animals Desertion." As she finishes, she almost chokes as she whispers, "Now that my ladder's gone, I must lie down where all the ladders start, in the foul rag and bone shop of the heart."

I kiss Mam goodnight, and hug her a bit tighter than usual, before kissing the Old Man's cheek. I leave them alone in the kitchen and make my way to bed, where in the darkness the room feels exactly like the rag and bone shop Yeats wrote about.

I toss and turn for half the night, under the Manchester United poster. At some point after I hear them go to bed, I slip out of bed and pad down the carpeted stairs to the kitchen. A noise stops me and I shimmy behind the half-open door and look through the crack.

The Old Man swallows the pills in the dark of the kitchen; his Adam's apple bobbing away as the gold-hued Power's washes them down. Mam keeps the whiskey under lock and key to prolong his misery, a private joke. I hear her tell Uncle Harry on the phone. "It's no picnic," she tells my uncle. "I put a notch in the bedpost each time he wakes from the nightmares and tries to strangle me."

He is what Mam terms, "a cute hoor," and he refills the whiskey bottle with tap water to where she's drawn a line on the label. He screamed at her last week, for measuring out the whiskey like, "an effing accountant." His fingers rattle the screw top shut. Under the potted hydrangea, he replaces the key and up the stairs he goes in short, heavy steps.

I retrieve the key and fetch the Power's from the cupboard afraid the creaking floorboards will wake the house up. I take a sip of the yellowish liquid and my mouth burns. Disgusting. The horrible taste makes me twitch and I knock the bottle over, the whiskey spilling into the sink.

I hold the bottle to the moonlit window to see how much water I must put back in the bottle to fool Mam and the Old Man. Upstairs, the bed groans from the Old Man's bulk and I hurriedly put the bottle back where it came from, praying to my Guardian Angel my deception doesn't get discovered.

I am shepherded into the dining room the next day, and the Old Man stands at the sideboard, the whiskey bottle beside him. The ledger of sins is on the table. "Tell the truth and shame the devil," he intones. "Tell the truth and shame the devil." He watches me squirm, hands behind my back, a half-cracked smile of guilt on my face. "You drank the whiskey. Didn't you?"

He writes my sin in the book and pushes the point of the pen into the paper with force. Nothing is worse than a liar in the Old Man's book. It is the trigger that sets his fists in motion. To tell a lie is to dance with the devil and get what is coming.

He has a sharp nose for falsehoods, and brings his splayed fingers down on my bare cheek in a wonderful split-second before the pain arrives. Sharp with denial, I smile wryly.

"It's for your own good." He utters his judgment. "This gives me no pleasure." His eyes glint as he metes out justice from on high.

The following morning the phone rings early and the Old Man spends a long time saying "Yes, yes, yes. Thank you. Absolutely. Yes."

"Well, there's a fine how do you do!" he says. "That was the gaffer from the rig telling me I'm to be promoted to driller when I go back for my next shift."

There's a brightness to his face and he's happier than I can ever recall in my life.

"Well may you wear it," Mam says, though I never quite understand why this is how we congratulate someone on good news.

He says, "We'll be on the pig's back now."

Mam says, "It's a blessing, and to celebrate we'll have roast beef and Yorkshire pudding."

"Sure, the job will put us on our feet again and back where we belong," he says. "We might even be able to afford a color television on hire purchase."

"I'll pay off our slate across the road," Mam says.

"You'll be able to hold your head up in this town from now on," the Old Man says, his chest swelling. He gives Mam a squeeze and kisses her forehead. I set the dining room table with the good cutlery. The silverware resides in an old, velvet-lined box, and age stains pattern the knives and forks. When Mam left her hometown the dinner service was all she left with.

The roast beef is the way the Old Man likes it; blood

pooled on the serving plate, and the Yorkshire puddings fat and burned crispy. There's a great aroma of roast potatoes and the sharp tang of horseradish sauce. He whets the carving knife, sliding it against the sharpener like there's a sword fight about to break out in the dining room. Mam opens a bottle of stout and before we eat anything she escorts Granny to the table and we say Grace.

The old woman starts the prayer. "Bless us O Lord, and these, thy gifts," then lapses into "Forgive us our trespasses, as we forgive those who trespass against us…"

The Old Man rolls his eyes at the mix-up with the Our Father, and Mam dabs at her eye.

Granny sits with us while the Old Man carves the remainder of the roast. She seems to be shrinking each day. I don't know how old she actually is, but wiry hairs stick out from her nose and they're whiter than white. Mam tells her to stop pecking at the roast beef because it cost a fortune, and Granny stares at her as if she's never set eyes on her before, and says, "Will we take the horses for a canter later?" She fingers the frayed edge of her dressing gown.

"Now, you know we've not had horses since the war," the Old Man says, twirling his index finger in circles near his temple when Granny looks away.

"Oh, no. I rode Lazarus to the lake the other day," she says, spitting a bit of meat onto the plate with a smile.

"Have you phoned the doctor yet like I told you?" Mam asks, giving the Old Man the sharp edge of her tongue. The rattle of his cutlery on the plate answers her question.

My shoes scrape the floor beneath the table and I wonder which of my parents I'm going to resemble when I get older. Mam says I have the Brogan ears and that there's no getting away from that. Sometimes I press my hands against them and try to push them back into my head, but all that happens is the blood pounds in my skull and my ears turn bright red.

For the rest of the meal we eat in silence. The Old Man

says young boys should be seen and not heard at the dinner table. The only other sound's the clicking of fork and knife, and the smack of satisfied lips.

After dinner Mam helps Granny to bed and the Old Man swans off to the pub to prolong his celebrations. I go into the sitting room and read the "Victor Yearbook" from last Christmas. I love the story about Billy Bunter and the boarding school where all they do is eat buns and play pranks on their teachers all the time. You couldn't do that at my new school because the teachers are savages from the depths of the bog and they're also quicksilver with the leather strap if you so much as look at them the wrong way.

Mam does the dishes, produces the laundry hamper from under the stairs, and sets the ironing board up in front of the fire. She turns on "The Undersea World of Jacques Cousteau," and we watch the *Calypso* sail the ocean blue, swarms of seabirds trailing the boat across the water.

"My fingers are worn to the bone," Mam says as she folds the Old Man's y-fronts into a neat pile. "Don't I have to take care of your grandmother as well as the two of you?" Cigarette smoke thunderheads around the fluorescent light as she sprays Robin's Starch on the ironing board. "Is it a skivvy you think I am?" she asks, stubbing the cigarette out on a dirty saucer.

I leave her to the ironing and head out to find my friends who said they'd be hanging out at the top of the lane. The cold makes me sneeze and when I can't find anyone I draw a whale on the red-bricked wall with a white rock. Inside the whale's belly I draw the Old Man and a skeleton sitting beside him sharing a bottle of whiskey. I've always wondered why skeletons always have large holes in their skulls where the nose belongs.

I get in from the lane and the Old Man is still not home. Mam packs me off to bed. After I brush my teeth with the striped Colgate, I pee into the toilet, kneel bedside and say my prayers asking God to not make my yoke hairy like the Old Man's.

Again, the Old Man disappears for most of the next day, prolonging his celebrations, and he arrives home that evening and says, "I have a bit of a surprise for you, son."

He waves us towards the front door, and when he opens it a tan-colored greyhound is tied to the railings.

"Da! Is it really ours?" I say. I've been begging him to let me have a pet for ages and all he says is no. But, when the dog turns our way there's a stump where its left hind-leg should be.

"Ah, for the love of Jesus, what in the name of God do you have there?" Mam asks. "Couldn't you have gotten the lad a four-legged dog at least?"

"Ah, woman, I was saving its life, because she was off to the knacker's yard unless I stepped in and bought her. So, this is your new dog, son," he says, rubbing the dog's head vigorously and clicking his tongue at it. "Bart Conway sold her to me for a fiver. Isn't she a grand old bitch altogether? I thought she'd make a fine late Christmas present, now we're going to be having a few more bob to spare at the end of each month."

"Ronan, the bloody dog has three legs! Would you buy a chair with three legs?"

"It's not the same. She's a thoroughbred," he says. "She'll make a great pet for the young fellow," he adds. "Come on over and say hello to your new dog," son.

"You're soft in the head. Who do you think is going to look after that poor unfortunate?" Mam lights a cigarette and blows smoke into the evening air.

I don't like that the dog has three legs, but it's got the nicest face, all narrow and pointed. "Where's it going to sleep, Da? Can it sleep on my bed, please?"

"For tonight, son. But you and I will build a dog house

out back tomorrow, and if you walk her and feed her each day, you'll get a few bob extra in your pocket money each week."

"Now, what should we name her?"

"Her racing name is Lord Kitchener's Revenge, but we'll call her DeValera, after that bitch's bastard of a president." He leads the dog into the house, leaving Mam to trail in behind us, puffing away on her cigarette.

The Old Man slaps the dog's rump and she turns a pointed head and nips at his hand. "By the hokey, there's life in her still!" he says, stroking her two long ears with one hand. He opens the back door and lets the dog off leash. She makes a run for the end of the garden, unhampered by the missing leg.

"If she ruins my garden I'll put the two of you out on the street," Mam says, rapping at the window with her wedding ring. "Go on, get away from the fecking phlox," she shouts at the dog, which ignores her and squats down to pee on the flowers.

The dog tears about the rectangular lawn at quite a lick.

"Can I let her in, Mam? Please?"

Mam relents and I open the back door and the dog races through the kitchen and makes for the sitting room, where it attacks the armchair and snatches the antimacassar that's covered in a sheen of the Old Man's Brilliantine.

"Ah, I'll be dug out of you. Get this bloody dog out of here," she says, flicking a tea towel at the dog's rear.

"I'll do it, Mam. Here girl, here girl," I cry, the dog cocking her head to one side. I slip the leash onto her collar and as I go to the front door, the Old Man pats my back and smiles.

"Do you know what? That dog better not turn out to be trouble, or it'll be straight off to the knacker's yard with it," the Old Man says, shaking his head.

"I promise I'll teach her not to destroy things, Da," I say. "She only needs a chance to settle in here and she'll be grand."

Mrs. McGeough lives at Number 8 on our side of the road and has a Yorkshire terrier, Sparkles McGillicuddy, who wears a tartan jacket all year long. The Old Man jokes that the name weighs more than the dog. Sparkles is at the gate, yipping away, and the two dogs bend over to sniff noses. I yank on the leash and keep going towards Terenure.

We take a left at Garville Avenue and head for Brighton Square and the little park opposite the house where James Joyce was born. Mam doesn't like to talk about the writer and his dirty books, and says he was a ponderous old drunk. Tommy, says there are "sexy" bits in the books and he bets my parents have copies hidden somewhere in the house. I searched Mam's old hat boxes, but all I uncovered was knitting patterns taped together and ancient black-and-white photographs of strange looking old people with big ears and sad eyes.

When we return from our walk, Mrs. McGeough is in the doorway with a bottle of skin cream in her hand. She has the same light green bottle of Ponds that Mam uses for her dried skin. "Tell me, now," she says, "When are we going to have a little rendezvous between Sparkles and that new dog of yours? They'd make lovely puppies together; don't you agree? And they might have four legs, too," she says, laughing at her own joke.

"Sorry, Mrs. McGeough, the Old Man says it's not good for her to get her dander up, in case she might go for the postman."

"Oh, God, that's right. Poor old postman, sure he's been limping these twelve months since Sparkles mistook him for my poor dead husband."

The Old Man drives by in the Austin looking for parking. He lowers the window and says, "Get that bastard away from DeValera before I throttle you."

DeValera dances in a circle, trying to leap on the car, but

the Old Man steers the jalopy away from us and keeps yelling. Sparkles races around the patch of lawn in the front garden, but Mrs. McGeough has retreated inside her house to hide behind her curtains, the ones covered with brightly colored fruit. She's motionless, but I can see her shadow, the nosy old bag. Once, she invited Mam and me for tea and her kitchen was drenched in water from the leaky upstairs bathroom. When Mam said something to her about getting a plumber, the conversation stopped and we all sat there like eejits. As she peeks out at us, I feel sorry for her and how lonely she must be with only the dog for company.

"Come on, girl," I shout, pulling the greyhound, her claws scraping the pavement. Sparkles squeezes out between the railings and tries to mount DeValera again, but the poor creature flails in mid-air. We escape along the footpath, past an ESB crew pouring new cement in front of our house, five collective legs moving in exact time. I don't like how much work taking care of a three-legged dog involves, and wonder if I've bitten off more than I can chew.

After the ESB workmen drive off in their van I finger my initials into the puddle of wet cement outside our garden gate, but I don't see the postman coming up the avenue with the sack of letters over his shoulder, and when he wallops me with his hand his Claddagh ring leaves a heart-shaped mark on my cheek.

"You bloody vandal, didn't those men spend their day setting that cement, and you deface it for fun?"

"Sorry, mister..." I say, and before I can go on, his hand loops around with a whoosh and clatters me on the side of the head once more. "Ow. Stop hitting me," I shout, as he pops letters in the slot in our door and straddles the low railing to get across to our neighbors.

Mam sees my cheek when I finally go into the house and

says, "What the blazes happened you?"

"The postman hit me for writing in the wet cement."

"God forgive me, what do you mean he hit you?" she asks. "I'll be phoning the General Post Office and lodging a complaint with them."

"Sorry, Mam. I was writing my initials in the cement for posterity," I say, using the word my teacher used in class when he was telling us about Padraig Pearse and the heroes of the Easter Rising in 1916. The great struggle for independence from the British always gets our teacher prattling on for hours. We've learned all about the signatories, who were executed in Kilmainham Gaol once the British suppressed the revolt.

"You're lucky your da's in the pub, or he'd tan your hide for your trouble," she says. "Go to your room until tea is ready."

After grabbing a can of Fanta from the fridge I run upstairs to the bedroom and lay under the poster of Georgie Best. I scatter my copies of *The Victor* comic on the bedsheet and ready for a marathon reading session. After a while I'm bored reading and ask if I can go out and play.

"No. You'll stay there and stew in your ignorance. I'm going up the village for the messages," she says, knotting the scarf under her chin. I crawl onto the window ledge, lower myself onto the roof of the garden shed, and shimmy down the wall like the Green Berets do in *The Victor*. I slip and a rose bush breaks my fall. The sharp-cut edge of a stem pierces my trousers and sinks into my bottom. Alone in the back garden, with no way back into the house except the way I came, I sneak out onto the road and make my way to the top of the lane across from the house.

Cathy and the girls are playing hopscotch on the chalked grid on the footpath. Four and seven are rest squares, and you can put both feet down before going on. From the corner of the lane I watch her in the evening sunlight. Her brown shoes are scuffed at the toes and there's a wrinkle in her burgundy school skirt. She goes to St. Louis in Rathmines now, and gets the bus early in the mornings. Sometimes I walk with her as far as the traffic light and then I make my way to my school, which is in the opposite direction.

She says it's okay if I want to take her to the flicks on Saturday morning. It's always a matinee in the Kenilworth Cinema and they're showing re-runs of Flash Gordon. The last time we went to the cinema I touched her face and it felt like the sand on the beach at Bettystown—all soft and warm. I was afraid to utter a word, but if we go this week I'm going to try and kiss her.

Cathy tosses the "Mansion" shoe polish tin onto the grid and hops, splits, and hops again before stopping onto the seven square. She's playing with Nettie Hanratty who doesn't like me at all. Mam says her parents are left-footers and not to be trusted. The two girls talk as they play and the stones in the tin rattle as they throw it on the grid. Cathy's wrist is narrow as a twig and the sun catches her watch and sends a stream of light toward the ground. There's a moment of silence as I linger at the corner, imagining the kiss we'll share on Saturday morning in the darkness of the Kenilworth. Cathy waves good-bye to Nettie and starts walking toward me.

She stops and asks me about the new dog, and I tell her all about the Old Man's promotion and how happy he's been since the news. She wipes her nose with the sleeve of her cardigan and scuffs the toe of her shoe on the ground.

"You look sad," I say.

"My ma and da got it a huge fight last night and he smacked her in the eye. Ever since my little sister died they've been at each other's throats."

"Sorry about your sister," I tell her. "Jacinta, wasn't it?"

"Jacinta, that's right. I wear a piece of her jewelry every day so I have something to remember her by. This barrette is hers," she says, pointing at a ladybird barrette in her hair.

We've lived here for ages and I heard her sister had died

of Leukemia, but it's not talked about around the neighborhood. I suppose when children die families don't want to discuss such things.

"Why did your da smack your ma?" I ask.

"She was down at the church stuffing envelopes for Father McDaid, and when she came home, Da said she had drink on her breath, and he accused her of using the priest as a cover for having an affair with someone." As she says this she twirls the end of her hair in her fingers and blushes.

I'm stunned at the idea of Mrs. Prendergast in some other man's clutches. I dream of her at night, and I know it's a sin, but I can't help myself. I tell Cathy that her dad shouldn't be smacking her mother at all.

"Well, she's always dressing fancy when she goes to the church, and that one time the priest tried to look down her blouse..."

What sort of woman Cathy's mother is at all? Does she really make an effort to make men pay attention to her, or is Cathy imagining that's something she does? Her ma is nothing at all like Mam, that's for certain. Cathy must be embarrassed by her mother's transgressions, and who might she be having an affair with? Maybe it's one of the other fathers on the avenue. Maybe it's the Old Man, and when he says he's going up the road for a pint, he's really meeting Mrs. Prendergast and having it off with her.

No. He's away far too often to be doing that. Mam would know. And I hear them doing "it," every now and again, so he doesn't need to be seeing other women.

After I say goodnight to Cathy I sneak around the back lane and climb over the garden wall. I scramble up onto the shed roof and climb in the bedroom window in the nick of time. Mam announces it's dinnertime, and before going downstairs the muslin curtain trails through my fingers and I can almost feel the softness of Cathy's hair. If Mam knew where I'd been and what I'd been thinking she'd skin me alive.

Chapter 6

The Old Man asks if I've been at his whiskey again. It wasn't whiskey, it's poitín: illegal moonshine made by his old friends in the Knockmealdown Mountains of Tipperary.

I shake my head. "It had mold on it," I say. "It's poison." The half-empty bottle glows in the light from the chandelier, and he curses me for thievery. I yell back at him, and purple in the face, he grabs me by the elbow and wraps me in a bear hug.

"Stop it, Da," I say. "I only used a little bit to clean the dust off my records. I read in a magazine that it's the best thing for keeping them in good condition."

My shouts bring Mam in from the kitchen where she's basting a goose for dinner. Her arms are crossed and her lips tight in anger. A smear of butter runs across her cheek and she wipes at it with her apron. "Let him go, Ronan," she says. He shakes his head and cradles me tight, squeezing until I squeak like a stuffed toy. "I said let go, he's just a child," she says.

"He's fourteen," the Old Man says, shoving me into the piano. "And he wasted that good poitín on those bloody records of his. I'll bloody well skull him."

The metronome rocks, upsetting the vases on top of the piano. Mam watches the shivering crystal-ware. "Oh, sweet Jesus," she says, as the tallest vase topples to the carpet and rolls to the leg of the dining room table. Another vase falls and the high-pitched ting echoes and Mam catches it before it hits the ground.

The Old Man goes for me again and this time I make a grab for his arm and the piano shudders.

Mam throws up her hands. "Why ever did I marry into your family?" she asks him. "I always knew you'd amount to nothing."

The Old Man slumps into the armchair by the fireplace breathing heavily. Mam collects the fallen vase and checks it for cracks. It has a large fissure in it and she cradles it to her chest and sighs.

"It belonged to my grandmother," she says, sitting down in a cane rocking chair and weeping.

The Old Man mutters dark words before going over to check on her, and I take the opportunity to flee to my bedroom.

At the dinner table the Old Man mumbles, "Sorry."

I sit down at my place and we eat in silence, the dog condemned to the yard. After the plates are cleared, Mam takes the custard out of the oven and brings it into the dining room along with the sherry trifle.

Mam places a bowl in front of him, the whipped cream spiky and snow white, and he gazes dreamily into the distance as a small trail of drool runs from the corner of his lip to his chin.

"D'you have a spoon?" he asks, and ever the gracious servant, she trots to the sideboard drawer for the silverware.

"What in the blessed world happened to my good

spoons?" She holds a crested spoon in her hand with an enormous bend in the middle.

"I was practicing my Uri Geller," I say, fidgeting with my hands. When Tommy and his cousin came over, we played mind-bending games with the cutlery. His cousin popped a pimple with one of the spoons and proceeded to twist it into pieces.

"Uri Bloody Geller?" The Old Man shouts, upsetting the bowl of trifle on the table. "Now look what you've made me do." He pushes the remains on the floor and there's a crash of breaking glass.

Granny calls down from her bedroom, "Ah, can I have some Complan, for the love of God?"

"I'll deal with you later," Mam says, getting to her knees and scraping the mess up with a sponge. "I have to take care of your blessed Grandmother. Sure, if it's not the pair of you I'm looking after, it's her I'm traipsing up and down those stairs for." Her face is pained and she rubs the back of her leg with her shoe. "Aren't the soles of my feet worn out? Have a bit of compassion, would you?"

Granny is bewildered, and that it's a terrible affliction for old people. He tells us a story at dinner about an old fellow from Athleague who went out his door one night and walked straight into the lake and drowned in minutes.

I eat my trifle in silence and wonder whether Granny would manage to drown herself in the pond at Bushy Park if she got out of the house without any of us seeing her leave.

"It's a bitter pill, getting old," Mam says, retreating to the kitchen to prepare Granny's dinner.

The Old Man reminds me of the spoons and I try to give him the slip. "I'm off to see Tommy," I shout.

"No, you're bloody well not," he bellows after me. "Get up those stairs to your room and don't come out until I say so. You'll come to a bad end, bending spoons like a fool."

He follows me and rattles the door handle, and I tie the

doorknob to the wardrobe, praying he won't break in.

The front door slams a few minutes later and I watch the Old Man head off up the road, bound for the Off License to get a bottle of whiskey no doubt. I give him a few minutes and crawl out the window, shin down the drainpipe, and make a run for the back lane. If I can get to town I'll meet the lads and maybe be able to avoid the Old Man until the house gets quiet again. That's what friendship is, I suppose; people you can go to when your life is about to turn out bad.

At the bus stop, there's a bee buzzing about my head and try as I might I can't kill it. Flailing at the annoying insect I realize I don't matter to my Old Man at all. He is nothing like me, either in temperament, or looks. He's almost featureless—like the Invisible Man. But unlike the Invisible Man he will batter me when he catches up with me.

I've been at the bus stop for half-an-hour when I realize the buses are running on a skeleton service because it's Sunday. Three 15Bs pass me bound for the terminus and deciding it's not worth waiting, I head for home. As I'm about to turn onto the avenue, I spot the Old Man coming down the road swerving from side to side, the brown bag sticking out of his pocket, and the sun glinting off the telltale gold cap of the Powers' whiskey bottle.

He doesn't remember the spoons and he collapses in in his favorite armchair the minute he gets into the house. The curtains are drawn, and the lights on. He's in the doghouse again and Mam is at the end of her tether as she likes to say.

The kitchen door rattles on its hinges and Mam stomps to the hall and changes from her apron into her Sunday overcoat, the one with the diamond pin shaped like a peacock's tail pinned to the collar. She dabs lipstick on her mouth and hugs me, the coat scratching my chin.

"I'm running off with a soldier," she shouts in at the Old Man, and pushes me toward the stairs. "Go to your room and play like a good fellow."

I pick at the edges of the pages in my book, rolling the torn bits in my fingers and saying, "I wish I was dead. I wish I was dead," repeatedly. Cats scream from the alleyway behind the house and a narrow line of ice frosts the windowpane. In shadows by the back wall a white cat limps towards the neighbor's garage.

I test the theory that there's another world on the far side of the wardrobe by putting on my anorak and tying the hood about my head. The plastic tassels on the hood are chewed to bits, marked by my teeth marks. I climb into the wardrobe, push past the clothes and Auntie Martha's cello and knock on the back panel. Downstairs the Old Man snores, chastened by Mam's threat to run away with a soldier. Nothing happens in the wardrobe and the hooded anorak muffles my sobs.

The kettle hisses steam into the cold kitchen and poor children die in Africa at the rate of five a minute. That's what Father Flanagan tells us at school when they passed out the Trocaire boxes during class. The Lenten Collection boxes are for our spare change and have pictures of thin-armed, dark-skinned children on all sides. There's a narrow slit for the money to go in and Mam glues down the flaps so I can't open it up and steal money to buy sweets.

For Friday afternoon's religion class, we watch a film of the children, millions of them, bawling, tubby infants with huge bellies and stick-like arms and legs. The hospital they're in is a big tent with "no air conditioning at all," according to Father Flanagan, and who reminds us he was on the Missions in Sierra Leone with some Greek priests. "'The White Man's Grave,' boys," he says, thudding his fist on the desk over and over. "'The White Man's Grave," he repeats. "Mind you collect as much money as you can for Lent, and God will know if you steal from the boxes."

He palms a mint into his mouth to disguise the smell of

the drink he's had for lunchtime. We always watch a film, or photo slides on the projector, on these afternoons. Mam told me he has a disease and can't help it, but when I remind her that the Old Man smells of drink often, too, she shakes her head and says, "You don't know what you're talking about."

"The capital of Ethiopia, Brogan?" the priest asks.

"Addis Ababa," I shout.

"Spoken like a genuine scholar," he says, palming another mint. Mam also says his drinking is not sustainable and when the headmaster finds him at it there'll be hell to pay. "Hell to pay," she says, over and over.

We barrel out of the school entrance when the bell rings, the weekend at last. I pedal like a madman all the way down the Terenure Road, past Our Lady's School, Bushy Park, the library, and Eaton's cake shop where we buy bags of broken cakes for pennies. As I cycle past my old primary school the church bell rings, and I spot Father O'Cuinn, our Irish teacher, inside the cage that protects the bell, his cassock blowing over his head in the wind.

I do my homework in the dining room, my books spread out on the table, the gas heater firing on all bars. I like to get it over with quick so I can spend the weekend doing fun stuff. Sometimes, though, I leave it till Sunday night and all the work due for Monday is rushed and sloppy.

After my homework is done I play records in my room. Most of them are 45s and I stack them on their sides, the covers facing outward. I have a paltry number of LPs: *Tea for the Tillerman, Goodbye Yellow Brick Road, and The Wild, the Innocent, and the E-Street Shuffle.*

The Old Man says I should buy some proper music, along the lines of Percy French, and Count McCormack. Mam laughs when he says this and sends him into a sulk which usually means a trip to the pub and a night of him singing "The Mountains of Mourne," half-scuttered in his armchair.

Across in the lane, the girls are clustered together, Cathy

tossing her hair and the other girls laughing with her. The curtains are almost opaque and they can't see me spying on them, which means I can keep looking at Cathy for ages. She's with one of her school pals who lives on St. Enda's Road. I never go near the place because of the gang of lads from there. "A pack of corner boys," according to the Old Man.

Friday means fish. Mam breads the fillets of plaice with the Paxo breadcrumbs and drops them into the sizzling pan. The radio dongs for six o'clock and she blesses herself and mumbles the opening lines of the Angelus.

"The Angel of the Lord declared unto Mary..." she intones.

"And she was conceived of the Holy Ghost," I add.

Her face is all concentration even though she's praying, smoking her cigarette, and cooking the dinner at the same time. We finish and she gets her purse, takes out a five pound note, and says, "Go over to the Dairy and get me twenty Dunhill" She presses the money into my hand and returns to the hot pan. Frying oil and cigarette smoke fill the air and sometimes if feels like we live inside a cloud.

Don Cockburn's voice is on the radio talking about fifty-two people dead on a flight in Argentina. Mam shakes her head and blesses herself. She wipes a tear from the corner of her eye at the thought of all those people dead in South America. The Old Man's snores drift down to the kitchen from where he sleeps in the sitting room.

The road is icy, and my breath forms clouds in the night air. I poke a hole in a puddle and break a chunk of ice off. Bits of dirt and leaves are trapped in the ice and a small insect has died of exposure, or drowning. Can you drown in ice?

I break the shard against the railings and an inch-long piece flies into the road. Instead of fried fish, I wish we were having pancakes for tea, with golden syrup and lemon, like we do on Shrove Tuesday.

The bell clangs above the door of the Dairy and Mrs. Dooley, red-faced behind the counter raises two bushy eyebrows at me. "What do you want, young Brogan? Speak up, young man."

She treats me as if she's one of my teachers, always going on about my soft voice, the way Father O'Cuinn yells at me about the conditional tense in Irish class.

"Twenty Dunhill," I say, handing her the note.

"Anything else?"

"May I have a roll of Spangles? The orangeade ones?"

She hands me the cigarettes and sweets. I head out the door sucking one of the sweets. The fizziness erupts when I crush it in my teeth, and the taste of the orange my favorite thing in the world.

When I get to the garden gate I pretend I am Captain Kirk from Star Trek, and hold the box of cigarettes to my mouth and say, "Energize." Nothing happens and I have to press the doorbell to get inside.

Mam is warming the plaice in the oven and the Old Man, resurrected, brings Granny's tray to her room. The radio is on and Mart and Market announces the prices of heifers. An ad comes on and the announcer says, "Leo Yellow Injector, gets rid of Mastitis."

"What's Mastitis?"

"Something cow's get in their udders," Mam says.

"How does something get in their udders?"

"Stop with the questions. Don't forget you've to go up to the church for your Confirmation rehearsal tomorrow."

After dinner, when Mam and the Old Man are dozing by the fire, I sneak into the hall where the Trocaire box sits on the gramophone cabinet with the telephone. My tongue is between my teeth as I gingerly try to slide a fifty-penny piece out of the slit. I'm skeptical about the babies and our money saving them. Instead, I taste cola bottles and bull's eye sweets. Fifty pence buy a grip of stuff at the sweet shop.

At the same moment as the ten-sided coin is in my fingertips the door opens and the Old Man grabs me by the shirt. "You feckin' lout. Stealing the money for the babies in Africa."

My squirming does no good and he batters me on the head until my ear throbs. I drop the box and it crumples on the floor.

"You bloody heathen. I'll teach you about hardship," he says, going for his belt.

"Ronan! Stop it." Mam holds his arm and pulls him away. "He'll pay it back. All of it," she says.

"Oh, I agree. He'll get no pocket money this side of Christmas," he says, his face purple, and as I pull away and make for the stairs he plants a foot in my arse that takes the breath out of me.

"Write the theft down in the ledger like a good woman," he says to Mam.

Before he can lay another hand on me, he's interrupted by Granny banging on the radiator in her bedroom with the metal potty.

"By Jesus, if she doesn't stop that bloody racket I'll go up there and suffocate her."

Mam rushes upstairs to see what's the matter with Granny. In the back garden the dog pushes her empty food bowl around the concrete and the Old Man shoves me toward the back door and says I'd better fulfill my obligations if I don't want another good thump.

The Tupperware of scraps rattle into the dog bowl and I tip the tin of Pedigree chum dog food on top of the mess, there's a horrible sucking sound as the jellied food slips from the can. The stench is brutal, and I curse the Old Man under my breath.

"Fuck. Fuck. Fucker."

Flies cluster on the rim of the bowl as DeValera licks the potatoes.

Before I can get in the back door there's a smashing sound and glass showers down from the upstairs window.

Granny is halfway out the open window in her nightgown. The Old Man bursts into the yard and shouts, "Get back in the window."

Mam is there, pulling her back, both arms around her waist. She is hysterical, screaming, "Ronan, get up here, for God's sake. I can't hold her."

I feel sick, and the dog goes mad with barking again.

"I'll murder that bloody dog," the Old Man says, as he flees upstairs.

I follow him to Granny's room where Mam is weeping on the bed, her arm around Granny. The Old Man knocks away the sharp bits of glass from the window and when I ask him about the dog getting injured he harrumphs and keep knocking glass shards into the backyard below.

"What if DeValera eats the glass?" I ask.

"If she does, it'll kill her. I'll have to call the glaziers before the weekend, I'll close the shutters until its fixed." the Old Man says.

Mam nods, while Granny rocks back and forth, her eyes wild and staring into space.

"I'd better sleep with her tonight in case anything else happens," Mam says. "And I'm phoning Harry immediately. I'm not able for this anymore. My heart is broken and I'll have a nervous breakdown if it goes on any longer."

"Don't send me back there," Granny says, and pushes away from Mam and toward the glassless window.

"Now, Mammy, it's only a phone call. No one is sending you anywhere."

Mam looks as if she's about to leap out the window this time, and the Old Man is sighing, which means he's about to lose his rag again.

Mam says, "I'll bring you up a nice cup of Complan and the "Woman's Weekly." She settles Granny in the bed again and calms her down.

The Old Man thumps down the stairs and the front door

rattles as he disappears off to the corner pub for a pint or two.

Mam and I leave Granny nodding off in her bed, and Mam shuts the door gently behind us as we leave.

The Old Man has left for the oilrigs again and Mam, Granny and I slip back into the familiar routine of companionable quiet. School drags on and Easter approaches and with it, Confirmation.

I'm a bit embarrassed to be making my Confirmation at almost fifteen. We usually do it between twelve and thirteen, but the Archbishop said something about how excited he is to be confirming the first "experimental" classes of older students. Father McDaid says it's because the Vatican thinks twelve or thirteen is too young for Confirmation, and we're the guinea pigs of older students, and we'd better turn out to be perfect Soldiers of Christ. Mam tried to stop them from changing the rules a few years ago when they announced the change, but Father McDaid brushed her off with a wave of his hand and told her to mind to her own business and let him tend to his flock.

Tommy is coming out his door and I wave at him to wait. We tramp to school along the Rathgar Road, down Airfield Road, along the back of Harrison's Row, and turn left on Winton Road. Streetlights hang from electric wires across the width of the road. They're dark green and look expensive. When we get to the end of Winton Road, we turn right at the corner of Terenure Road East, where in the autumn we collect fallen chestnuts for the conker wars. We keep going until we reach Jonesy, the Lollipop Man.

Jonesy holds a round stop sign and wears a white coat like our doctor. He's old, with frizzy white hair and a bushy moustache. He is the kindest man in the world, and has twinkling brown eyes, and he helps us across the road each day with his slow, limping walk.

We are good collectors of money, and despite being poor; we always have a few pennies to go to Carroll's Sweet Shop, where even ten-pence can buy a dozen bull's eyes and twenty cola bottles. My favorites are the orange creams, the ones that melt like butter in your mouth. Each time I eat one I savor each second and make it last until nothing's left except the memory.

Two doors up from Carroll's sweet shop is Dwyer's Newsagent's. This is a massive shop with toys, magazines and books.

We're reading the magazines on the shelf when Tommy dares me to steal a copy of the *Wizard* with a gift inside. I stuff the comic down my jumper and close my coat tight.

As we're about to head out the door someone grabs me by the collar. I know the woman. Her name is Biddy. She's a mean little yoke with Penelope Pitstop glasses and teeth that stick out at angles. Her eyes are two squinting pinpricks in a moon of a face.

"Call the Guards, Mr. D!" she yells.

I try to escape and wriggle free eventually, taking off out the door and heading straight across the street into the busy traffic, dropping the comic on the pavement behind me. I run all the way home to the relative safety of my bedroom.

When the phone rings later in the afternoon, Mam answers. She puts on her "telephone" voice when she is talking to someone. "Yes. No. Thanks so much, Biddy." The phone clicks when she puts the receiver back in the cradle.

My ear-tips are bright red when she arrives in my room. She wears her blue overcoat buttoned to the top and a colored scarf tied under her chin, brown stockings and shoes.

"Did you steal a comic? Did you?" she says, banging me with her hand. The edge of her wedding ring gouges at my head and hurts something awful.

"Yes. I'm sorry, I won't do it again. Tommy made me."

"By God you won't. Wait until your father gets

home, my young buck. Put on your coat now." She marches me along by Carroll's and past the display of Easter Eggs, chocolate rabbits, and furry yellow chicks in the window. We go into Dwyer's Newsagents and Mam marches up to Bridie and Mr. Dwyer. They're not too happy. Mam gives them a good telling off. I stand behind her, hands stuffed in my pockets. When we come out she propels me forward, her hand on my schoolbag. "That's the last of our business they get," she says. "And you, my lad, have my heart broken."

Mam lights a cigarette in the kitchen and hangs her coat under the stairs. I complain that I won't have any comics to read on Friday after school. Usually we get them from Dwyer's and I spend the evening stretched out on the floor, reading the *Wizard, Victor, Shoot,* and *Topper. Woman's Weekly* for Mam, and *Salmon and Trout* for the Old Man. This week I'll be comic-less and forced to re-read last week's with Tommy.

She scowls at me and storms up the stairs to her bedroom. The door to her bedroom rattles on its hinges and she bangs about in her room for a good while. Finally, she comes out with a suitcase in one hand.

"I've bloody well had it with you. I'm running away with a soldier."

Granny asks from the bedroom, "What's all the commotion about?"

"Ah, never you mind," Mam says, grasping the suitcase in her hand.

She marches downstairs and takes her coat from under the stairs, stands at the hall door, the long blue overcoat buttoned to the chin, floral headscarf tightly secured, and her hard, brown suitcase at her feet.

"Don't go! Please," I plead. "I'll be better. I promise!" My heart is banging and I know she's only moments from leaving for good. What will the Old Man say when Child Welfare sends for him on the oilrig?

She pulls on her Dunhill cigarette, the end flaring red in

the dim hallway.

Her hand goes to the latch. She cracks the door and the cold blast of air hits me like a hard slap of the wooden spoon.

"Aaah, I promise I'll be good." I make one last plea for clemency, the tears flowing down my face.

"Jesus, Mary, and Joseph," she says, pulling the door shut again, taking her coat off and hanging it back in the closet under the stairs. The suitcase is carried upstairs and slid under her bed. I disappear to my bedroom in utter silence, barely able to catch my breath.

I have new clothes for my confirmation; blazer, shirt, tie, and gray slacks. Mam says I'm a smasher, and I wish I agreed with her, but there are big black hairs between my eyebrows and they're driving me crazy. Tommy says I've a unibrow, like that Mexican woman who painted strange pictures of flowers and trees. I take a safety razor and shave a gap in between my eyebrows.

Mam is hopping mad when she sees what I've done. "You've ruined yourself. Jesus Christ, wouldn't you be better off leaving your poor face alone?"

"Sorry," I tell her, and give her a hug.

The Old Man can't get off the oilrig for the occasion, and said something about a new gas field further north of where the oilrig he works at is located. Mam is disgusted and tells him so. It doesn't matter because I'm used to him disappointing me. I do get a card and a twenty-pound note from him, and another card from Uncle Harry and Auntie Martha with two twenties inside. Mam shakes her head. "Straight into the Post Office savings account, my lad," she says.

I want to buy a bird book and new binoculars, but she won't hear of my plans.

The church is packed, and we're all dickied up in our blazers and ties. The girls from Our Lady's Convent are making their confirmation with us, and they're all in white dresses, veils, and shoes. Lots of the girls have white lace gloves and matching prayer books with gold crosses on the cover.

The archbishop is at the top of the church and he's going to bless the lot of us. I want to be paired up with Cathy, but instead, when the time comes for us to approach the altar, I'm opposite some spotty-faced girl with thick glasses. We kneel and are blessed. When the mass is over we all form a procession down the aisle of the church to the outside where we're going to have our photos taken by the school photographer.

We go home for tea and cake and some of Mam's cousins arrive and press money into my hand. Later, I go around the avenue to visit the neighbors and collect even more money. Mam insists I put all of it in the Post Office, but when I don't stop begging for a bird book, she relents and says I can have five pounds for books, and justifies it because it's educational.

Nobody says anything about my shaved eyebrows and I go to bed that night full of sherry trifle and roast pork. Mam makes my favorite things, and her cousins stay to dinner. I hear them say something about miscarriages when they talk to Mam. What if she's already had a baby who didn't live long enough to arrive in the world. She has been going to the doctor, and she's always picking up prescriptions from the pharmacy. I never ask what her medicine is for, because I know ladies have problems that men don't have, and it's best not to interfere.

I dream of the summer holidays and the beach, and searching the sand dunes for bird's nests. My farts are terrible and I wake up to a room full of poison gas and can't get back to sleep. I can hear Mam in the next room crying out the Old Man's name. I stay where I am and try to ignore her.

Tommy and I sometimes attempt to steal some things from the Dairy, waiting for Mrs. Dooley to turn her back and fiddle with the radio, or when she goes to the back door to let a deliveryman in. We take petty stuff: chocolate bars or rolls of sweets, easy to conceal under a shirt or behind a back.

Sometimes we run messages for the upholsterers who have a workshop in the lanes behind the avenue, up at the back of Golden's house, abutting the Murphy's back garden. Benjy, Dermot, and George are constantly stripping the covers from couches and chairs, refinishing the furniture with velvet and velour coverings and always listening to BBC Radio 1's pop music. Benjy is a longhaired twenty-two-year-old who is apprenticed to the two older men in the workshop. Much of the time they sit around reading the *Sun* or *the News of the World* and looking at the nude page three girls and their huge breasts. We're in and out of the workspace bugging them and asking them what they're doing to the furniture.

Benjy asks myself and Tommy to run across to get some Kimberley Mikado biscuits for the afternoon tea. He's a bit of a thick and seems to be as dense as soup. While we wait for the men to find their change, one of the older ones whispers to Benjy who says, "Will you boys get me a packet of French Letters, too?"

His workmates snicker and we go off to the shop to get their messages. Tommy and I wander amongst the shelves, eating Tayto Cheese 'n Onion, the oily residue getting all over our hands and clothing.

With the Mikado on the counter, pink and white spongy goodness with raspberry jam in the middle, Tommy asks Mrs. Dooley for the French letters. Her face deepens to a purple hue and a trail of spittle flies from her mouth. She yells, "Get out of the shop and take your dirty ideas with you."

We haven't a clue what she's on about and run across to the workshop with the biscuits for the workmen's tea.

"Where are the French letters?"

"She wouldn't give us them," Barry replies.

"Ah, for God's sake, I'll have to get them myself then,"

Dermot says, laughing. We disappear into Tommy's back yard to play some table football in the garage. We haven't set up the players before his ma comes from the house and marches into the garage. She looks unhappy.

"Which of yiz were over at the shop looking for French letters?" She folds her fatty arms across her chest and glares at the three of us.

"I did, Ma," Tommy replies, scratching his neck and looking guilty. I say nothing, and stick my lower lip out further than my upper one.

"D'yeh know what they are? Do yeh?" she asks.

"No, Ma," Tommy says.

She clatters him on the head and asks where he heard of them. "Benjy asked me to get them with his biscuits." At this point she storms off, slamming the garage door behind her and telling us not to move. We follow her at a distance and eavesdrop as she screams herself hoarse at the three wise men in the workshop. We catch bits of her angry words, "Ashamed of yerselves, wait 'til your father gets home and he'll deal with yiz, dirty old men…"

At the mention of her husband's name there's complete silence. Tommy's da is a bullish man with not much of a way with words, but a real means of getting his message across. His kids know the ability he has with his fists and often arrive to school with fresh bruises on their arms and faces. Granted, some of the bruises would have been at the hands of Tommy's mam as much as they would have been from his da.

Anyway, Benjy tries to talk his way out of the situation telling her, "Ah sure Missus we were just joking with the young fellas."

She snorts and replies, "Joking? When my husband finds you, there'll be some joking to be dealt with and it'll not be you that'll be doing it, mark my words." She shepherds us back into the back garden and shuts the door behind her with a bang.

We return to our table football and after an hour or so

Tommy's da roars from the kitchen.

"Jaysus, now lads, there'll be fireworks in the back lane," Tommy declares, rubbing his hands together and grinning like a maniac. Sure enough, his da storms out the kitchen door in his white singlet, his crazy gray hair waving in the breeze, lips tight and fists clenched. Tommy's ma follows him and we leave the shed and trail behind them.

"Which of youse sent my boy to buy French letters?" he yells at the upholsters. The men are bent over sofas stapling material and pretending to look busy. Benjy lies under the chassis of a Ford Cortina that's up on two small jacks, the rear tire flat as a crushed Coke can.

"Who was it? Huh? Who was it then? Which of yiz did it?" The denial rings silent in the lane. Tommy's ma pulls Tommy's arm and asks him to point out which one of the men had sent him looking for the French letters. He points under the car.

"It was him. Benjy."

His da hammers on the hood of the car with his fists. Benjy begs him to stop but he keeps on beating the hood and shouting at Benjy to get out from under the car.

"I'm not getting out. You'll fecking kill me."

"I'll fecking kill you either way, you gurrier," Tommy's da says. He kicks at the rear jack and the car wobbles. He keeps on kicking at the jack and Benjy's screams increase. The car lurches and dips at the rear. Benjy scoots to one side. Tommy's ma is scared and pleads with her husband to come away from the car. He ignores her and starts kicking at the other jack. The two other workers implore him to leave their workmate alone. Tommy's da's oblivious to their pleas and keeps kicking and kicking at the jack.

"Stop! Stop! Police!" Benjy pleads. The older of the other men heads for the phone on the workshop wall.

Tommy's ma tugs at her husband's vest to pull him away from the car. "Come on, come on, leave the fecker alone," she begs.

We laugh at this point, thinking the whole scene hilarious. "Shut up and go back home," Tommy's da yells.

We simmer down in a hurry and slink back into the garden. In a few minutes, his parents come in from the lane, both red-faced. They're talking low and not at all happy. We keep out of the way and play a few more games of table football before I leave by the front door.

Mam is making the tea when I go into the kitchen, and I ask her, "What are French letters?"

"Jesus, Mary and Joseph, where did you ever hear of such a thing?" She declares.

I tell her Benjy's story and about his special "messages" he asks us to get for him and her brow furrows. I repeat my question and wait for an answer.

"Now, there are some things you're better off not knowing at all in this life," she says, scalding the pot with hot water. "You're growing up too fast for my liking, my boy."

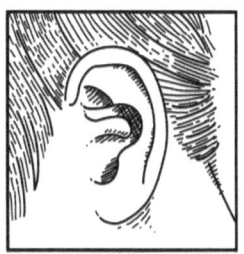

Chapter 7

Mam fries bacon and sausages for breakfast and says that this will be Granny's last day with us, as she's going home to Athleague. Mam says it's too much to take care of The Old Man and me, as well as an old person losing their marbles. The Old Man eats his breakfast in relative silence, save the crunch of the bacon and Mam's crying. He's strangely quiet and I know he doesn't want to see Uncle Harry. After he finishes his last bite, he takes off through the back door to work in the garden.

I'm not going to school today because I've got to see the doctor and have some earwax removed. I've been having whistling and ringing in my head for a few weeks, and Mam says I have "Tinnitus." I don't care, because I get to skip school and miss a boring visit from the Holy Ghost Missionaries, who are recruiting for young people to join them on the missions in Sierra Leone.

"A renewal of faith," Father McDaid said in school on Friday.

I don't want to go to Africa and work with the pagans and the cannibals. I want to be a naturalist like Gerrit Van Gelderen. I love his TV show, *To the Waters and the Wild*, and I want to wander the country searching for hidden creatures and discovering the beauty of the countryside.

I try to focus on my book report about *The Man-eaters of Tsavo*, a book about these lions in an African safari park. The report is for a school competition and there's a £20 book voucher as the prize. What must it be like to be attacked by a huge creature with paws the size of car-wheels? How fast do they strike their prey, and do they sneak up on explorers in their safari tents and watch the shadows inside until the right moment comes to pounce?

I've borrowed the book from the library. It's all about a man who helped build the Uganda Railroad through British East Africa and the lions who killed many of the workers. Some of my book report comes from the inside jacket of the book and I am careful to change the words so as not to arouse the judge's suspicions. I hope I win because the prize will be presented in front of the whole school and I'll have to wear my nice grey slacks and give a speech.

Mam says I'll make a good fist of the essay, and that I must make sure to spell words correctly, because those things count for the judges. She makes tea in the good teapot. "For luck," she says.

After I've been writing for an hour or more, Uncle Harry rings the doorbell. He says Auntie Martha stayed at home to get the house ready.

"Why is Granny going away," I ask Mam. "Don't you love her anymore?"

"Of course, I love her." Mam sobs and blows her nose with her handkerchief. "She's going to live with Uncle Harry and Auntie Martha at their house in Athleague," she says. "She'll be more comfortable there, with the view of the river and a few of her old friends still about. And your uncle and aunt have more time to devote to looking after her. I have enough on my plate taking care of you and your father."

The Old Man comes in from the garden and says a few words to Uncle Harry and gives Granny a hug. "Mind yourself, now. And don't be out gallivanting all over Athleague at your age."

He disappears out the front door and heads up the avenue towards the village, and probably the pub.

DeValera barks like ninety in the back garden, tormented by the O'Malley's cat that sits on the garage roof licking its paws. Uncle Harry helps Granny to the car, even though I want him to stay for tea. Mam says he should get on the road with Granny so she can get to bed as soon as possible.

I give Granny a hug, the bristles on her chin poking into my face. She pats my cheek with her hand and says, "God Bless you, and keep you from harm." She stoops to get into Uncle Harry's passenger seat, and once she's buckled in I wave to her, Mam's hand on my shoulder.

"Tell Auntie Martha I said thank you for the confirmation money," I say.

Uncle Harry baps the horn of his car twice as he pulls away from the curbside. Mam grabs me close. "What if I never see her again," she says.

I'm afraid I'm going to break down, but I'll be brave for Mam. I don't know what to say, and instead hug her tight and inhale the cigarette smoke and perfume trapped in her wool cardigan.

The Old Man staggers in the door later in the afternoon and says, "I suppose your brother is in Athleague by now? That'll be the end of her, and make no mistake." He flops into his favorite chair by the fire, and Mam bangs her book shut, slamming the door so hard the windows rattle.

After we've eaten, the Old Man says, "Will we go up the road to the 'Diggers? I'm panting for a drink, and aren't these my last few nights on dry land for an eternity?"

"And leave the lad here?" Mam replies.

"I'd like a drink with my wife tonight, for the love of Christ. And isn't he old enough now to stay in the house on his own for an hour. And now your mother's gone she won't need you for anything," the Old Man says. "And don't you need some consolation?"

"I'll put my coat on and we'll be back in no time," she says. Mam washes the crockery from our tea in the sink and goes into the closet to get her coat and scarf.

I wait for a while before slipping into their bedroom to open drawers and search under the neatly folded clothes for anything of interest. I know the large drawer under their wardrobe mirror should have something worth finding. The brass handle is a bit stiff and I use both hands to force the drawer loose. If the Old Man discovers me here he'll batter me stupid.

The bleeding heart of Jesus dangles over their bed and the light from outside washes over the eiderdown. It's not as if I'm looking for anything special, but there are two books under the heavy linen in the drawer at the bottom of the wardrobe. One of them is *Everything You've Ever Wanted to Know About Sex, but Were Afraid to Ask*, and the other is a book of dirty Irish limericks and the cover has some of the creatures from the Book of Kells doing some filthy things.

I open a leather-covered box hidden in the folds of a linen tablecloth. Inside, a small silver chain link purse holds seven coins. "Brogan," the name on a small slip of paper says. They must belong to the Old Man's mother. They're old, and have Queen Victoria on them. Treasure. Sovereigns, half sovereign, florin, farthing, and thru 'penny bits.

I take the coins and purse and after I shut the drawer carefully, making sure to arrange the linen the way I found it, I go back to my room. They'll never notice the empty velvet box. Maybe I can take the treasure on our summer holidays, bury it in the wilderness, and dig it up again next year.

My Guardian angel torments me to put the coin purse back where it belongs, but I shake my head and she disappears with a shake of the hips and a flap of her wings. The fear of getting caught tempts me back to their bedroom, but I want to make a treasure map like they had on Blue Peter last week. Peter Purvis and John Noakes drew a map and steeped it in tea bags for a while, and when they dried it with a hair dryer they burnt the edges with a match and it looked like the real thing. Lesley Judd said that we should only do it with adult supervision in case we burn our houses down. She looks like the waitress in the cafe up the village, except with a bigger nose. I stuff the purse and the coins in the bottom of the wardrobe where Granny's things are stored.

We eat porridge and toast while the news is on the radio. Mam switches it off and says, "We have some news to share with you, Patrick."

"Now, Son, we love you so much, and wanted to let you know there's going to be a new baby coming in the winter," the Old Man says.

The bottom of my stomach feels as if there are round boulders moving across it, pressing on my organs, making me want to vomit. I'm confused because none of the kids my age has parents who are having babies. I thought I was going to be the only one in our house. Now I'll have to share everything with another kid. "That's great," I say, hugging Mam and then the Old Man. "Will it be a brother or sister?"

"A little girl would be grand, but we'll have to wait and see what the stork brings down the chimney," Mam says, bringing me back into the kitchen and the Old Man's crunching sounds.

I'm a little excited there'll be a sibling for me to order about and do things, the way the Old Man bosses Mam about, but I know well that there's no stork, the same as there's no

Santa Claus, and that the Old Man had to put his yoke inside Mam to make the baby. Tommy says "gee" is a dirty word that means "vagina" and to make sure no one hears me use it.

I wonder about Cathy from across the road, and whether she has any hair on her vagina? Since the summer I've been getting some hairs around my mickey, and the Old Man says that it's a sign I'll be a man soon, and ready to give any young one I fancied a "lick of the gidean."

When he says "gidean" Mam screams. "God forgive you and your dirty ways. It's a long way from the gidean you were raised."

When I ask what it is, the Old Man winks and says he'll tell me at a more appropriate time. "You're still a bit young, and won't it be me your mother skelps with the wooden spoon if I keep corrupting you?"

"I'm going to be fifteen soon. I won't say a word to Mam," I say to him.

I'm not sure what happened, but lately I've had weird sensations in my mickey and when I rub the top of it with my thumb, it gets all tingly and a mad shiver runs through my groin. I know it's self-abuse, and Father McDaid says such behavior is the "Sin of Onan," but I can't help myself. He also said if we do it we'll end up as blind as Carolan the Fiddler.

I fidget about, my hands in my pockets, wondering about Cathy and her private parts as the Old Man tries to give Mam a squeeze. I've got the horn and I rub myself between my fingers. What if Cathy said it was too small, like a grasshopper? I can imagine the stuff coming out of it when I'm done, like a fountain, and I must look funny because the Old Man interrupts my daydreams with a clip to my ear and shoves me towards the front door.

I'm home from school sick and the Old Man is at the dentist's and Mam is doing the messages up the village. The kek kek kek of heels on pavement brings me to the window, where I see Mrs. Prendergast walking to her house, high heels clicking rhythmically. She wears a tight skirt and dark stockings and I can barely breathe.

I wait a few minutes and sneak downstairs, pick up the phone and dial the Prendergast's number, holding my breath.

"Hello? Hello?" Her voice crackles on the line.

"Uh, uh, you're lovely," I mumble into the receiver, all warm and moist from my mouth.

"Stop that. Don't call here again, or I'll set the guards on you," she says.

A sharp pain rolls across my lower belly and the front of my pajamas dampens. Just as Mam's key rattles in the lock I leg it upstairs and pull the covers about my neck and pretend to be asleep. Mam comes into the bedroom and puts a bottle of Lucozade on the bedside table. Along with the drink she hands me a *Warlord* comic and a packet of Tayto Cheese 'n Onion.

"Go on now, that'll keep you out of trouble," she says, placing a hand on my forehead to feel my temperature.

"You're more yourself," she says.

I nod, reading the speech bubbles in the first story, still aware of the dampness in my pajamas.

"You'll be fine to come downstairs for your lunch," she says.

I smile at her as she takes my tray with her, and recalling the thrill of hearing Mrs. Prendergast's voice on the phone I am aroused again.

Under the eiderdown I tremble, the heat stifling and heavy. I am shy, mostly not looking adults in the eye, mumbling responses to their questions and feeling my face redden. But the image of her stockings, the seams running down the backs of her legs, the static electricity when her skirt falls to the carpet, makes me want to go to the phone again just to hear her voice. Mam is downstairs, so I cannot use the phone.

I put my hand inside my underpants. *Linda. Linda. Lindaaaaaa.* Mrs. Prendergast's name soaks into the dark space and when *it* happens again my toes stretch to the bottom of the bed and I moan as carefully as I can.

Seducing Mrs. Prendergast is the mission I have accepted and in silence I try to plan how this will happen. Maybe she will wear a velvet cloak and come running to me like Maria in *The Sound of Music*? Or, perhaps I will knock at her door and ask her to sponsor me in the 5k walk the school is putting on for the Concern charity. Her husband will be watching boxing on television, and Cathy will be out at hockey practice, and her mother will take my hand and lead me to the bedroom, all perfumed and sweet, where she will put her lips against mine and run her hands all over me. We shall need good timing in case Mr. Prendergast hears us. Silence is golden, and we shall be quiet as mice as she fumbles with my trousers and I put my hands on her diddies. If he catches us he'll butcher me.

The Old Man says Mr. Prendergast is a muck savage from County Cork, and doesn't deserve a woman like Mrs. Prendergast. Mam has no time for her at all because she sometimes wears outfits that she declares "Brazen."

When the Old Man sees Mrs. Prendergast on the road in her fancy clothes he says, "By God, she's hot on her leather."

Mam sighs and bites down hard on her cigarette when he says things like this. "Mutton dressed as lamb," she says, snorting at the Old Man.

I jump out of bed and change into dry underpants before Mam calls me for lunch. At school, they're working on the angles of equilateral triangles, and reading some Latin text about Julius Caesar. I throw a plastic dart at the bull's eye target on the toy dartboard on the back of the bedroom door and go back to bed where Mrs. Prendergast's skirt waits in my imagination to be unzipped over and over and over again.

The stink of bleach mixes with Mam's cigarette smoke

and fills the kitchen as she boils the Old Man's underwear on the AGA. The bubbles peep over the top of the saucepan as Mam crushes her cigarette in the glass ashtray and empties a saucepan into the sink. It takes a nailbrush and hard scrubbing to get out the darkest stains, and she listens to the radio while she scrubs.

The doorbell rings, and Mrs. Golden from number seventeen handbags her way into the kitchen, a mesh shopping bag filled with onions and carrots hanging on her arm. Paddy Reilly, on the radio, sings about, "stealing Trevelyan's corn," and the kettle whistles high-pitched on the hob. Mam and Mrs. Golden are examining the rose bushes. Mam has the secateurs in one hand and the cigarette in the other.

Mrs. Golden's handbag is on the kitchen table, wide open. Her purse sticks out, and with one eye on the garden and one on the purse, I snap it open and pluck a fiver out. Later I'm going to go to Hot Wax and buy some singles from Charlie. Maybe I'll get, "I'm Not in Love," by 10cc.

When Mam and Mrs. Golden come back inside I'm given minestrone soup and hot, buttered toast, whilst the two women drink tea and talk about how to grow more scented roses.

We don't get thunder and lightning much, but today it's so loud the neighbor's cats are scaling the wall between our houses as if it's a cliff-face. When they panic and dangle in mid-air from the wall, does it cause their nails to fall off? Cats are funny ones, Mam says, and she's always dug out of them for urinating on her hydrangeas.

Charles Mitchell on the radio says, "A football match between a Derry Brigade side, and a Brandywell/Bogside team will take place this weekend at the Brandywell stadium in Derry."

At the stove Mam blesses herself. "What a waste of bloody

time," she says. The look on her face is stony. The laundry blows in the wind over on the O'Malley's line—the brown nylons, the white knickers.

I'm sleepy, having stayed up late reading under the covers. I like to dangle a torch from my knees and tent the eiderdown so I can read in the dark.

Mam declares that I'll ruin my eyes if I keep reading by flashlight. "You can't trick me," she says, ladling the lumpy porridge into bowls and pouring fresh cream on top. "I know you were reading under the sheets again," she says.

I feign innocence, grab my lunch from the fridge, and take an apple from the fruit drawer, and before I can head out the door, Mam shouts at me to make sure I'm wearing my scarf.

"It's pelting down out there. Wrap up warm for goodness sake," she says.

The scarf is knotted about my neck and when I pull on my waterproof leggings the seam rips and there's a big hole in the arse of the pants. If I didn't have an exam in Science class today I'd go on the mitch and play pool with the lads at Banjo Patterson's in Ranelagh Village.

Pedaling in the rain is hard work and the spray from the back wheel kicks the water onto my back where it trickles down through the rip in my leggings. I'll be saturated by the time I make it to school. Old Mrs. Dempsey is at the door of her house smoking a ciggie as I cycle past. The Old Man said she used to be a pin-up girl in the fifties. Now, she's a lonely old woman with a hooked nose and a miserable husband, who she says, used to love her. When she waves my way, I nod and keep pedaling through the pissing rain. I want to get to school early enough to finish my English homework.

When I arrive at the school gates a crowd is milling about, shouting and laughing, because the pipes have burst and there's water all over the gaff, so school is canceled.

I want to phone Cathy and lick mint ice cream off my

spoon instead of doing more boring schoolwork, but her school hasn't got the day off. Mam says I've got to do homework and study, even if school gets canceled, and that it's like practicing the piano; I've got to put in the hours. Sometimes I don't understand what she's talking about and wish she'd leave me alone and let me be.

When I'm finished with lunch Mam says, "Go out and enjoy God's fresh air now that it's stopped raining." She tells me to take my anorak in case it starts up again, and taps the barometer in the hallway, saying, "It looks like a change is coming."

I stick out my chin and bite my lip hard. I hate the stupid anorak with the furry collar, and when I get to the top of the lane I remove it and stuff it in the boot of the abandoned car beside the wall of the plant hire yard.

Tommy walks towards me and waves. He's been grounded for the past week because he ripped up his sister's Osmond's poster after she said the Undertones' album was shite.

We cycle over to the abandoned house next to Lahart's Garage, hunker by the old sycamore tree in a tangle of weeds and brambles, and peer at the old Edwardian house, its windows cracked and broken. We usually play soldiers in the lane, pretending to be commandos, scaling walls and trees in search of guerrillas.

"Did you see it?" Tommy says suddenly, pointing at the old house.

"What?"

"The shadow. The shadow in the bottom floor room!"

I look again, and sure enough there's a gray shadow inside the window, moving slowly back and forth. "It's a bleeding ghost!" I say, grabbing Tommy's arm.

"There are no ghosts, only dismembered corpses," Tommy says. "Come on. Let's get closer."

He drops to his hands and knees and scuttles toward the house. Afraid of being left alone in the abandoned garden, I follow him. We move rapidly, hoping nobody in the neighboring houses sees us and tells our mothers. We make it to the porch as the heavens open and the garden becomes a river of mud and slime. I'm soaked to the skin. Tommy pushes at the back door and it cracks open.

"Don't go in," I whisper.

"I'm not going to get any wetter," he says. There are rat droppings on the floor and dust an inch thick, and I reluctantly follow him, and for a laugh grab his neck with my wet hand. He screams and there's a door slam.

"Leg it," Tommy yells, barreling out the door.

In the rush, I snag my sleeve on a jagged bit of wood. Mam will have my guts for garters when I get home soaked to the skin and my jumper torn.

We scramble into the abandoned car, hearts banging, Tommy laughing his arse off. It's stuffy and smells of pee. The tinkers sometimes sleep in here, and cigarette butts litter the floor. Tommy pops open a bag of Tayto Cheese 'n Onion crisps, and I grab a handful. The crunching matches the patter of rain on the car roof, and when we're finished we lick oniony fingers and "Eenie Meanie" for who gets the inside of the bag.

"Let's go back into the house, it's barely sprinkling now," Tommy says. "It was only a door shutting in the wind."

"What if it's really a ghost?"

"Don't be mental. There's no such thing." Tommy grabs the rations and clambers out the window.

Back in the bushes we watch the house for signs of life, but the only thing that moves is a curtain blowing in a broken upstairs window. As we squat in the undergrowth the wind picks up and big drops of rain fall. Tommy makes a run for the door and I'm behind him in the familiar role of second-in-command.

An outdated calendar hangs from the wall in the darkened kitchen. *October 1971*. The Ford Cortina Mk. III in the picture is no longer on the market. The Old Man used to drive one back in the old days.

"Come on," Tommy hisses, pulling at my torn sleeve.

I try the sink to see if the faucets work. Nothing but a trickle of rusty water. Tommy's already halfway up the stairs when I get to the hall.

I'm shitting bricks. The house is quiet, though, no sign of whatever we heard earlier. At the top of the stairs a door is ajar and Tommy leads the way. There are tea chests, some without lids, some unopened. Most of them have the names of cities stamped in letters on the side: *Peking. Guangzhou. Hong Kong.*

We pull out plastic-wrapped decks of playing cards, fountain pens, diaries, and even bags of marbles; stuffing our pockets as if Christmas has come early.

Tommy goes through a stack of papers and forms on a table in the corner of the room, searching for cash. All he finds is a few 20p coins and a dull two-penny piece.

"That'll get us a bottle of Nash's Red Lemonade if we're lucky," Tommy says, as he pockets the coins and taps his fingers on the desk.

"What's in the other tea chests?" I ask him.

"Let's find out. I bet it's the good stuff," he says. As he wedges the lid off one of the closed tea chests another door slam comes from somewhere deep in the house.

He drops the lid and we flee the house, jump on our bikes and pedal off at full speed.

Chapter 8

When someone we know dies we burn a candle in the window and draw the blinds halfway down so the house looks like it's napping.

"The Bird is dead."

That's what the Old Man says when he reads he obituaries in the back of the paper. Mam nods, and the kitchen is silent for a long time. The clamor of a trapped mouse changes that and he raises the rolled-up Irish Independent over the creature, all furred and tense in the trap. The mouse makes frantic and the Old Man brings the paper down with a thump. A trail of yellowish red trickles from its body and Mam shakes her head and goes to get the brush and pan to clean the floor.

"Who's the Bird?" I ask.

She ignores me, pouring bleach on the sticky mess, wiping the guts up with a J-cloth. There's no school because it's a Holy Day; the Ascension of Our Lord, and the Old Man is home from the oilrig for the month of May. He has gone for his captain's hat, the one he found on a coastguard ship last year. The bells for Mass have already rung out, and it looks like he won't linger this morning.

"Go with your dad," Mam says, pushing me towards the front door where the Old Man is already blessing himself from the Holy Water font. It takes a minute to untangle my school scarf and pull on my anorak and then I run down the road after him. Mam has gone back to the kitchen to clean the dishes and prepare lunch.

"Who's the Bird?" I ask again.

"Ach, some old boyfriend of your mother's. He was planning on marrying her, until I showed up and beguiled her."

He adds, "Oh, the Bird was hopping mad when she began to court me, by God." There's a funny look on his face, as if he's smiling. "I took your mother out to Inch Strand and gave her a rub of the relic and that was the end of it." He claps his hands together and winks at me.

When we get back from Mass, I ask Mam what a rub of the relic means. She smacks me on the ear and tells me to mind my manners.

We leave to visit Granny after lunch because it's a Holy Day of Obligation. We haven't been to see her in ages and I can't wait to wander about Uncle Harry's shop. He has lots of toys and comics for me to investigate.

Out the window of the car, the passing fields, black and white Friesians, good milking cows, go by. The miles flee beneath the wheels of the Austin Wolseley, and the familiar signposts flash by: Kinnegad, Tyrrellspass, Clara, Horseleap, Moate, Athlone, Carrick, Lackan, and finally Athleague.

The streets press in on one-another, three-story houses rising gaunt and gray out of the barren midlands. Our car is stuck in traffic and crawls along the High Street; the evening Mass crowd briskly walks along the narrow footpaths toward the small Catholic Church. As the car pulls up the Old Man shouts, "Hurrah for shite!"

Mam curses. "Jesus, Ronan, I'll be dug out of you."

The house isn't so much a house as a series of rooms above the family business, a newsagent's shop where Mam was born, escaped from, and eventually returned to like metal to a magnet.

The three of us cross the busy street and enter the building. Uncle Harry waves at us. He looks like the big picture of my grandfather, turned against the wall in the spare room at home. Auntie Martha comes out from the back and hugs Mam and me, and shakes the Old Man's hand.

"Helen, grand to see you!" Harry kisses Mam as he speaks.

"Ronan, welcome back. Is everything well with you? How are things in the North Sea?" He grabs the Old Man's hand and shakes it three or four times, turning his attention to me and adding, "Patrick. How you've grown! Isn't he a grand lad now, Martha?"

"You're a topper," my Aunt says, smiling at me.

Maybe if we spent more time visiting them things would improve between the Old Man and Harry. Mam says it's petty jealousy on the Old Man's part, and that he hates the fact that Uncle Harry loaned us the money to buy the house in Dublin.

"Come on through, come on through. I'll have one of the girls put the kettle on for us." Harry summons one of the shop girls over from the counter. She disappears ahead of us, leaving the shop floor and we follow down a dark corridor lined with tea chests on one side and pictures of boats on the other.

Uncle Harry goes up a rickety staircase and into the bedroom where Granny rests, propped up by a half-dozen pillows, a knit cap on her head. The curtains are drawn shut, the air camphor-thick. She kneads the rosary beads and mutters "Hail Holy Queens," and "Our Fathers." I know she never ventures outside, save to be driven to Sunday Mass. She looks like one of those old women in the Grimm's Brothers' stories, ready to lure you into her lair and chew on your bones.

Behind the headboard, on the wall, the Sacred Heart of Jesus holds a flaming heart between his hands. Off to the side, a large bureau with five long drawers, and on top several framed pictures of my grandfather. There's that smell again, the same smell as in Granny's old bedroom—oldness.

"Helen? Helen? Is that you?" Granny's croaky voice wavers in the musty air.

"Mother, it's me. How are you?"

"Grand. I'm having my tea in the Royal Hotel with Mrs. Sheehan later. Will you come?"

Mam chokes back tears and smiles. "We will, of course."

Harry whispers, "She hasn't left the room in the month she's been here, except to go to Mass last Sunday. The doctor says she's comfortable. It's as much as we can do for her."

"Could you help me to the commode?" she asks.

The way Mam helps her get out of the bed and find the floor with her feet makes me incredibly sad. Granny shuffles over to a wooden chair with cushions on top. Mam lifts the cushions and a hinged piece of wood comes up to reveal a porcelain bowl. I turn away and peer into the cobwebbed corner of the room. When the dribble of pee finishes she helps Granny back to bed.

"Patrick, come here like a good lad." Granny's bony hand reaches out to me.

"Hello, Granny," I say.

"My mother and I didn't always see eye to eye. When she didn't kill me forty times over I was very lucky." She continues, her eyes sparkling. "On a brilliant summer's day you could almost see as far as Clonmacnoise. And in winter the floods came up and you might as well have been living in a lake. I loved it."

I look at Mam, not knowing what Granny is talking about. I bend over the bed and peck Granny's cheek, sucking in my breath at the strong scent of chamomile and camphor.

Her face is stubbly, like the Old Man's when he doesn't shave.

She grips my hand in her birdlike fingers. I pull away and move to the window. The shutters are not quite closed, and through a crack, the gray Shannon water laps at the end of the garden, a chink of light filters through and its slivered tip rests on the bed. The river winds its way through the fields at the back of the house. The backyard has a slipway that leads to the water's edge and Uncle Harry's dogs run hither and tither, chasing out-of-reach water birds.

We stay for an hour or so, having an awkward tea with Auntie Martha and Uncle Harry, finally saying our goodbyes and crossing the road back to the darkness of the church parking lot.

On the drive home, the meal rumbles around my stomach and I reflect on the misery of Granny's new life. The sliver of sunshine piercing her body stays with me like a scab on a cut knee. I dream later of camphor-scented trees and swinging bodies with stocking covered feet shining in the moonlight.

The prize ceremony for the book review competition is today, and the whole school assembles in the auditorium to hear the headmaster read out the winning names. I say a prayer to my guardian angel that I'll be one of the prizewinners and it'll be a fantastic early birthday present for me if I manage to win one of the three prizes. They're all cash, and I desperately want the school year to end in triumph.

The girls from Our Lady's School join us in the auditorium, because the competition was open to students from all the local schools.

Father Tubridy climbs the stairs at the side and walks to the center of the stage where he proceeds to give a speech about pride and honesty and achievement. Everyone claps and then the principal of the girls' school makes an almost identical speech. At least hers is a little funnier, but I'm so nervous I can't laugh.

The winners are announced in reverse order. A girl from the convent gets third prize and her classmates scream with delight as she accepts the envelope from our principal. Second prize goes to Dominic Gleeson from third year. His pals go nuts and chant his name over and over. The principal yells at them to shut up.

I'm holding my breath and my head feels strange as the principal opens the envelope for first prize.

"Brogan. Patrick," he announces.

Kevin bangs me on the back so hard I lose my breath and stumble into the chairs in front of me. Red-faced, I walk to the center aisle and head up to the stage. Father Tubridy and the Mother Superior shake my hand, and the nun gives me the prize. I'm mortified to be in front of both schools, scarlet-faced and with my unibrow shaved off. I can hear a few, "Wanker, Wanker," cries from my classmates, but I pretend not to hear.

Mam is thrilled to bits and phones Uncle Harry that evening to tell him the news. The Old Man says a little learning is a dangerous thing, but that I'm a great man for the letters altogether. It hurts me that he doesn't say more. It wouldn't cost him anything to say how proud of me he is, or that he loves me. Instead, he diminishes my achievement and tells Mam he's taking her to the pub later for a drink to celebrate and they'll bring me back a bottle of Club Orange if I'm a good boy while they're out.

We have a special dinner of rissoles and chips to celebrate. Mam fries the balls of meat and onion in the same oil as the chips and we eat them with Heinz beans. I pour tomato ketchup all over my chips and guzzle everything on my plate before the Old Man can reach over and fork my last rissole onto his plate.

While they're at the pub I am in charge of the house, and the Old Man says if I burn the place down he'll skin me alive.

I don't say anything, but if the house burns down I'll be dead already and he won't be able to do anything to me either way.

He puts a hand on my shoulder and says, "This is your chance to earn back our trust. Don't act the maggot."

I wait five minutes for them to walk far enough away, and then I go into their bedroom. I take a closer look at the sex book I found before. No pictures—at least not nudie ones—more's the pity. The bit about chastity belts confuses me. The Old Man hasn't told me about the birds and the bees, but Tommy's filled me in on the essentials as he knows them. Tomorrow is my fifteenth birthday and I've started sprouting hairs down there. The Old Man says when I'm ready to shave he'll tell me all about the birds and the bees.

I choose a pair of stockings from Mam's drawer, disappear into the toilet with the book. The bottle of Old Spice aftershave monitors me from the shelf with the red, yellow, orange ducks. I flick the pages and loop the pantyhose over my penis. It looks like a narrow-necked bank robber. I channel my thoughts into Mrs. Prendergast's naked body under me. The drawing in the book identifies this as the *Missionary Position*. After ten minutes on the cold concrete there's a small puddle on the ground. When I remove the pantyhose my thing is a bluish color and I'm afraid it might be broken.

I see more of the small black hairs on the wrinkled skin and decide to grab a razor and shave them off. I slip Mam's lavender-colored razor from the cabinet and remove the bits of hair. I jump at the rattle of the key in the latch downstairs and leg it back to the bedroom, stuffing the stained stockings in the back of Mam's drawer, making sure to scatter the clothes in the drawer over them.

I examine myself in the dark, using the flashlight. My penis looks like one of those salamanders in the zoo, all wrinkled and soft. I recite an "Our Father" so Mam won't discover the ringed evidence of my sin. "...And Deliver us from all Evil. Amen," I whisper, looking guiltily into the eyes of St. Martin de Porres, whose statue is on my bedside table.

A birthday card sits on my plate at the kitchen table and under it is a large oblong box wrapped in blue foil paper. Mam plonks my bowl of porridge in front of me and pecks me on the cheek, saying, "Many happy returns, Son."

"You're getting to be a big lad," the Old Man says. He ruffles my hair and kisses me on top of the head. Mam made him stay a day longer so he could be home for my birthday. I know they were fighting about it in the sitting room the other night because I heard the Old Man shout something about pulling anchor without him, and that he'd be having to stay an extra day on the other end of his shift.

"Can I open it?" I ask, eager to rip the paper off the present and see what they've got me for my birthday.

"It's your day. Go ahead."

Mam rattles the black and white pudding around the frying pan and I tear the card open first. "To our darling boy on his fifteenth birthday," it reads. "All best wishes, Mam and Da." The card has a monkey holding a bunch of colored balloons. Inside the box something is wrapped in tissue paper. I open the paper to find a royal blue polyester Adidas tracksuit like the one Gerry Peyton the Irish goalkeeper wears. The three white stripes down the arms and legs are great, but when I open the jacket properly it doesn't have the Adidas logo. Instead, it has a white circle with the name, O'Neill's. It's not Adidas. I smile, my eyes filled with tears, and say, "It's great, thanks!"

The Old Man says, "We'll go to Dodder Park today and kick the ball about. Just the two of us." The kitchen clock ticks loudly, and the near silence is deafening. The Old Man has never played soccer with me—not once. Forgetting the disappointment of the tracksuit logo, I run to the bedroom and get changed. On the way downstairs, the post falls through the letterbox and there's a card from Auntie Martha and Uncle Harry.

Inside their envelope, there's a crisp £20 note. I'm rich, and even though Mam will make me put it in my Post Office Savings book, along with my Confirmation cash, I'll be able to spend some of it on new books. Added to my prize money from school I'll have £120 in my account.

"Sit down and eat your breakfast, Mam says, placing rashers, sausages, pudding, eggs, and fried tomatoes in front of me.

The Old Man is halfway done before I can even eat one sausage.

"Can we go to the park after breakfast?" I ask.

"Let me shave and read the newspaper first," he says, mopping the egg up with a triangle of toast. Mam stands over the stove smoking a cigarette and drinking her tea. She raises her eyebrow at the sound of the Old Man sucking his false teeth.

We walk up the village past John of God's and the Garville Arms Hotel, the soccer ball clutched under my arm. The Old Man has no soccer gear and wears his brown brogues, the ones with the holes punched in the front. At Dodder Park we take a left and make for the soccer pitch.

"Right, then." The Old Man puts the ball on the faded penalty spot and walks back four steps.

I stand in the center of the goal and crouch down like Gerry Peyton does on the telly. There's no grass in the goal-mouth and small pebbles and rocks litter the ground. He takes a run at the ball and toe-pokes it at me. I'm able to block his shot, but my hands tingle from the power of it.

"Great save," he says, trapping the ball and replacing it on the spot. An old lad and his dog watch us from the footpath.

The Old Man takes a run at the ball and sends it to my left, and I dive toward it and miss. My knee scrapes the ground and when I stand up there's a scuff on the polyester, some threads ripped.

"What's wrong with you? Would you get the bloody ball?"

"I ripped the knee, Da," I say.

"Arrah, are you a man or a mouse? Stop your sniveling and play the game."

I want to abandon match, and sit in front of the fire with a book instead, but the Old Man won't have any of it. We play on; him kicking penalties, me not diving for fear of making the tear in the knee worse. After a while the Old Man tires, his face reddened from the exertion, and we head back. In the village, we stop at the newsagents and he picks up a free copy of *The Sacred Heart Messenger* and slips it into his back pocket.

Mam is on the phone when we get home and she waves us towards the kitchen. The Old Man slips into the sitting room and when I come back from the kitchen with a slice of apple tart, he's already asleep.

I lick the apple off my fingers and pick at the knee of the tracksuit, still wishing it were the official Adidas one. I bet the Adidas one wouldn't rip from one simple scrape. Georgie Best looks at me from the bedroom wall in agreement. He looks proud in his Manchester United kit, and I pray one day I'll be famous like him.

The Old Man is off again tomorrow, so we have a special dinner for my birthday at a nice restaurant in Rathmines. There are linen napkins on the tables and the waiter wears a shirt and tie. Mam says, "It's not just any day you turn fifteen." So, I'm allowed order whatever I fancy.

Somewhere between the prawn cocktail and the boiled tongue my pimples flares up and causes Mam to drop her fork and exclaim, "Oh, Jesus, your poor face is destroyed." She wipes my chin with a bit of wet tissue paper and says, "There now, you're game ball."

Whether it's the Marie-Rose sauce on my cheeks, or the

red pimples that have sprouted on my face, Mam says not to put a finger on myself until she washes me with a wet cloth and applies some of the Sloan's Horse Liniment—the Old Man's cure for all maladies— from the common cold to the Black death.

The Old Man works a piece of gristle between his false teeth and growls as he struggles with the meat. As I lick the sauce from a prawn he resorts to putting the knife in his mouth to pry some meat from his teeth and Mam sighs. He raises a bushy eyebrow and continues to worry away, daring her to say something.

"How many valves are in a prawn's heart?" I ask, afraid that I'm eating all sorts of queer organs I know nothing about. I resist the urge to scratch my pimples and fork another prawn with its dead heart into my mouth.

"I haven't the foggiest notion," she says. "But I do know their hearts are on top of their heads."

"God, that's fantastic," I say, amazed at all the wonderful things she knows. She learns lots of them from her set of Everyman Encyclopedias on the bookshelves in the dining room. I love the green covers and the gilt numbers on the spines of the encyclopedias, or is it encyclopediae? Father Flanagan said something about Latin plurals ending in –iae in class a while ago.

When we go home I want to explore the volume that has lots of stuff about astronomy, the formation of suns and how they travel through the universe at dizzying speeds. The Old Man is our angry sun, and we orbit him like two helpless planets.

Tommy and I decide we need to go back to the old Edwardian house. We're petrified of getting caught, but we really want to explore what's in the closed crates.

Tommy says. "I'll lob a stone at your window round midnight."

"I don't know. That old fellow might be dangerous," I say.

"Don't be a scaredy cat. Be ready at midnight," he replies, heading out my bedroom door. I watch from the window until Tommy reaches his garden gate and goes inside.

I grab a jumper and pull it over my shirt. Georgie Best looks down from the poster over the bedside table. He's a wild one, too, with his Beatles-style haircut. Down the stairs and into the kitchen I go, taking the steps two at a time. Mam makes Birdseye fish fingers and baked beans for tea and the windows are all steamed up.

"Where were you at all? Have you done your homework?"

"Yes, Mam. I did it the minute I got home."

"Don't try to pull the wool over my eyes, fellow me lad. Just because your da is off at sea doesn't mean I won't take the wooden spoon to you and fracture your backside." She spits the words out between clenched lips, the cigarette smoking away.

"No. I promise it's done."

She coughs, and stirs the saucepan. "Sit down for your tea."

She ladles beans onto a slice of toast, and forks two fish fingers on top. Sometimes I pretend the Old Man is Captain Birdseye, a jolly fishing boat captain, instead of a grumpy oilrig worker. He must get awfully lonely out there in the middle of the North Sea. He talks to us once a week and says a few words to me before he talks to Mam, but mostly he's making sure I'm not getting into trouble. He never asks me about how school is going, or what sports I'm playing.

After tea Mam does the dishes and banks the fire with slack before she settles in for the evening with her Dame Ngaio Marsh book. The cover has a sultry lady in a fancy ball gown. I mooch about in front of the hearth reading a new Arthur Ransome book, and when she sends me to bed I'm unable to sleep, knowing Tommy's going to be looking for me at midnight.

A pebble clinks the windowpane and Tommy's in the front garden waving me down. Mam's low snores come from the bedroom and I tiptoe past her door in socked feet. The landing light is on and I make my way to the front door and silently unlatch it.

"C'mon," Tommy hisses, "We've got to get up the lane. I have a torch."

The night is warm and the walls of the lane sparkle in the moonlight. The house is in darkness, no lights in any window, and we make for the garden, the beam from Tommy's torch showing the way. I'm tempted to turn and run home, but he grabs hold of my sleeve and tugs me along.

Inside, the place is creepier than during the day and a mouse runs across the kitchen floor. Tommy jumps and knocks against the door.

"Ssshhh!" I elbow him in the ribs. We wait a minute for any noise upstairs. Light from the lintel about the front door casts a silver hue in the hall, the clouds have cleared and the moon is finally out. We creep up the carpeted staircase past crooked paintings and peeling wallpaper. The door to the room we were in previously is open and Tommy shines the torch on the crates. He half-disappears into the first open tea chest. When he emerges he's in possession of a handful of bones. "Jesus, look at this! A skeleton!"

"What if he's a murderer?" I say, my whisper too loud.

He waves the long bone in his hand and I step backwards and fall over another crate.

Tommy motions for me to be quiet.

"We need to get out of here," I say. "Those are human bones!"

"No, they're fake!" he says, smacking me on the head with one. "It's plastic!"

Shuffling outside the room send us into the shadows. We wait for the man to find us in the darkness, but all we hear is the door shut with a loud click. The footsteps fade away and Tommy moves to the door. "He's locked us in." He sweeps the beam from the torch all around as if there might be another exit.

"Trapped, yiz are. Ye little gurriers," says a voice from the other side of the door. "Yiz can stay there overnight and reflect on yer sins."

"Let us out mister," Tommy shouts. "We're sorry. We'll never come back again."

Silence. Tommy tries the doorknob again. Locked. We are frozen—surrounded by tea chests, plastic skeletons, salt shakers, ladies' nylons, and other bits and bobs—stuck in a room with a madman on the other side of the door keeping us hostage.

"Will he kill us? Maybe he's the Son of Sam's Irish cousin?" Tommy says.

"Shut up. Let's see if we can get out of here," I say.

From the window, we eyeball the drop to the ground. It's a long way down and there's no drainpipe to hold onto.

Music from somewhere. Dickie Rock and the Miami Showband, and a voice singing, "At seventeen it's a thrill to dream someday you will walk hand in hand from the candy store to the chapel on the hill."

"Hey," Tommy says. He's wearing one of those old flying helmets from World War I, the kind with the earphones attached.

"Come on. Stop messing around. We need to get out of here."

"Look above the door. There's a cracked open window," Tommy says.

The glass lintel is hinged, but it's too narrow to get out.

"Flash the torch in the keyhole," I tell him, an idea forming. The key is in the lock and I do what I read once in an Enid Blyton adventure and slide a sheet of paper from one of the crates under the door, and use a chopstick to push the key out of the keyhole. The carpet muffles the sound and when the key appears under the door Tommy hugs me in triumph.

Slow, slow, slow, the key turns in the lock until it clicks.

"Come on," I say, "Let's scarper."

"Hang on, after all this trouble we deserve some reward," Tommy says, filling his canvas carry bag with fistfuls of playing cards, marble, and other things.

"Here, what's this?" Tommy holds up a bunch of black and white negatives. He covers one of the negatives with the flashlight and we see a naked woman in a bathtub wearing a shower cap.

Tommy flicks through the remaining negatives. "Yeah, all dirty pics!" He shoves them in the bag and we sneak to the door. We can make out snoring from somewhere and creep down the stairs in the dark. Once outside we barrel for the wall.

"I'll stash these under my bed," Tommy says, waving the negatives. "You'd better take half of them," he says, holding out a bunch. I stuff them in my pocket and head for home.

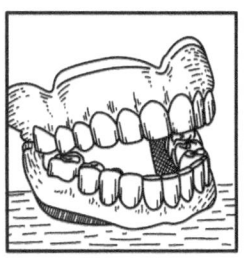

Chapter 9

School is out in a week or two, and we don't know what to do with the dog when we're away. The other day she stole a fresh loaf of bread from the cooling rack and when the Old Man tried to take it away she tore into him with her claws. Now he has long scratches on his arms and declares that he'll declaw the *Fianna Fáil* bitch, if she'll stand still long enough. DeValera is as slippery a customer as her human namesake, and limps out of harm's way any time the Old Man gets close.

The one time he does manage to grab the dog by the collar, she buries her teeth in his hand, causing frantic scenes in the kitchen. Mam pours Mercurochrome on the wound and bandages it in a clean tea towel. I hide the dog in the coal shed until the Old Man's anger passes. When I take her out for a walk later, she's covered in coal dust.

I'm reading in my room when Mam arrives in from the shops and finds the Old Man asleep in his favorite chair and DeValera gnawing on his false teeth. It takes a good half hour to finesse the teeth from the dog and not wake the Old Man.

Mam finally frees the teeth, soaks them in Jeyes fluid and works them with a Brillo Pad to take out the teeth marks.

The Old Man finally wakes up and finds his teeth chewed to bits and goes mental. "I'll swing for the bloody bitch," he roars.

I slip out the front door with the dog until the Old Man's temper cools, but I'm afraid he's going to get rid of DeValera. At the 15B bus shelter I sit down on the cold bench, put my arms around the dog's neck and tell her I won't let anything bad happen to her.

I see Cathy Prendergast on the way home and ask her if she wants to come over later to listen to some records. She says she'll try her best to get out because her parents are fighting again and she hates the atmosphere in their house.

I get back to the house and put DeValera in the back garden with a bone from the butcher's shop. Because poor old DeValera is banished, I bring her bed out to the coal shed. The Old Man insists on her not spending another night in the house. I sulk and storm upstairs to my room, where I sit at the window and stare into the fog for signs of ghosts. The electricity pole outside the house is almost invisible and the light glares orange in a halo.

If I could get out of the house and up the lane to the tree house we built from twisted branches and stolen planks of wood, I could wait for the spirits to appear. The Old Man has me on a short leash though, and instead I go downstairs to read *The Swiss Family Robinson*. Soon I am away in the world of shipwrecks and tree houses, my ghost watch suspended.

Mam is exhausted and goes off to bed early. A little while later Cathy arrives from across the street. I invite her in and we slip under the kitchen table, which is covered by one of Mam's long tablecloths. As we're sitting on the linoleum chatting about school, footsteps sound on the stairs.

The Old Man, face-crumpled, stutters his way across the kitchen floor to the bread bin. He reaches a calloused hand behind and rattles the lid of the bread bin with the whiskey bottle, and a "feck" comes from his lips. "Poor Old Dicey Riley, she has taken to the sup," he croons over the unscrewing of the Powers Gold Label. "Poor Old Dicey Riley, she will never give it up."

Cathy squeezes my arm and giggles. I hiss in her ear and smell her neck, bitter with her mother's perfume. The bottle re-screwed, bread bin closes, and the soft soles of the Old Man's Hush Puppies squeak back upstairs.

"I'll show you mine if you'll show me yours," Cathy says, and pulls her plaid school skirt up, revealing her butterfly underpants.

"Go on, then. You first," I say, barely able to breathe.

She pulls the waistband away from her tummy and reveals a line of hair the same shape as the line Mam makes on the top of the bread before she bakes it in the oven. I try to put my finger there but she smacks me on the hand and says, "Give us a look." Fumbled zipper. Limp and damp. "It's like a worm," she says with a laugh. She reaches out a finger along its length, her jagged nail tickling me.

After she's gone I wonder if what we've done will send us both to Hell. I'm petrified to tell Father McDaid at confession, because even though he's sworn to secrecy because he's a priest, I know he'll batter me silly when he sees me around the playground at school. I wish the Old Man had told me more about all of this stuff.

Anything sexual is a mortal sin unless you're married, and the priests tell us we'll go to Hell if we succumb to temptation. The lure of the flesh is a terrible thing according to Father McDaid, and he suggests boys wear as tight underwear as possible to diminish the excitement. I'm not sure whether he's right or not, because Cathy says she's caught him trying to look down her mother's blouse when he made his house visits at Christmas. I don't blame him, to be honest, because priests are men, too, and Mrs. Prendergast is a smasher.

We've been counting down the days to the end of the year in our school planners. I've got big red Xs through the days and today I put a giant exclamation point next to the final X. Too bad there's a storm brewing in the Arctic that's supposed to bring cold weather for a week. Typical. At least we don't have any major exams like third and sixth year students.

Tommy and I have planned plenty of adventures already and I can't wait to get home and put my uniform away for the summer. Some of our teachers put the brakes on our plans and make us do school work on the last day, but the fun teachers let us drink lemonade, eat crisps, and have free time instead of working. I suppose they're as excited about having their holidays as we are.

The sixth-year students won't be back though, and they loiter outside the bathrooms waiting to trap younger kids in the jacks and flush their heads in the toilets. I can't wait until I'm that old and can boss the younger kids around. Maybe I'll get to practice on my new sibling when he or she is old enough.

The bell for sixth period rings and we whoop and holler, some kids throwing journals in the bin on the way out. I keep mine, though, because I've got plans for it. I'll see Tommy over the summer, but the rest of my classmates can go take a running jump as far as I'm concerned.

Some of the teachers are at the gates saying goodbye to students, but most of them are in the local having a glass of whiskey and saying good riddance to bad rubbish. Tommy has a theory that teachers are like vampires and retreat into their coffins for the summer. This might be true, except that Father Tubridy celebrates Mass sometimes, so he either leaves his coffin for an hour or two, or Tommy is mistaken.

I have to fold my uniform and put it away until autumn and Mam examines my jumper for holes in case she needs to darn it before next school year. I wish she'd let me have one of the ones they sell at the school, because theirs have necks that don't sag, and sleeves that don't stretch. But we don't have much money and Mam saves a bit by knitting her own clothes.

"I suppose you'll be counting the days to school again," she says, with a teasing laugh.

"Yes, Mam. I wish they had school all year long, too."

"Go on, away with you and enjoy the freedom. It won't last long at all."

Emboldened by the thought of no more school for three months, I decide to rob the shop across the road when it closes. I got the idea from a television show I saw on ITV last week, and if I can get some extra cash I'll be able to sneak it into Mam's purse so she can buy some nice things for herself and the baby.

I am waiting for the last customer to leave the sweet shop before I try and steal the money from the register. Mrs. Dooley is half-blind and if I linger until after she closes the shop I'll be able to stuff the notes and coins in my pockets and escape out the small window at the back of the shop. I also need the cash to buy the Airfix model of an experimental racing car I saw in Hector Grey's toyshop last week.

Rows of Bramston Pickle and HP Sauce line the shelf, and I stick a bag of Dolly Mixture in my pocket for later. The bell over the door tings and Mrs. Dooley fumbles with the key in the lock. From my hiding place, I see the frayed shawl on her shoulders shake as she haucks her guts up. She smokes like a chimney; a Woodbine cigarette always dangles from her lips and she drives the smoke out her nostrils. She shuffles back to the counter and opens a packet of Cream Crackers and bites off a corner. She counts the money in the drawer and scribbles in a long, narrow ledger like the ones we use for commerce class at school.

She shuts the register and sighs. Her voice breaks into a

gritty quaver and she sings, "The Blue Hills of Antrim, I see in my dreams. The high hills of Antrim, the glens and the streams..." The next thing I know she's wiping the tears from her eyes with the corner of her shawl. Something inside me cracks and I want to cry, too. She heads to the back where she lives behind the shop, leaving me alone in the dim light. I can't believe the prim old lady who never says more than two words to me is a secret songbird.

Her tears won't permit me to steal her money. Instead, I stuff a packet of Tayto Cheese 'n Onion crisps down my trousers, sneak over to the store room and climb out the small square window as her voice pipes out of the darkness, "The Blue Hills of Antrim I see in my dreams. The high hills of Antrim, the glens and the streams. In the sunlight and shadow, in weal and in woe. The sweet vision haunts me wherever I go..."

Tommy and I decide to search for bird's nest in the tall trees at the top of the lane, because we are only days into the summer holidays and we are bored with the routine of games of three-and-in with the Golden twins, and trips to the old quarry to swing over the water in the inner tube that hangs from a high tree branch. It's not that we are missing being at school, but we need to stay busy, to keep moving, so that we "Expand our horizons," as Mam says.

Mam summons me from the front door to come to my tea, her voice carrying over the rooftops to the narrow lane. At the same moment, I spot a small nest in the crook of the sycamore we've climbed. There are twigs and bits of thread woven together, and when I reach out to touch it a small furred chick pokes a head out. Eyes dark as velvet, it chirps sharply, "Tik-tik-tik," and my finger touches its head. Mam's cashmere cardigan, the one she got for Christmas from the Old Man, is what it feels like.

Fragile, all feathers and bones, the chick is alone, except for a single unhatched egg. "Maybe it's an orphan?" I say to Tommy, who straddles the branch opposite me.

"It's like a peach," he says, cupping it in both hands.

"Put it back!" I say, worried that the mother will reject her offspring, because that's what my *RSPB Field Guide to Birds* says will happen when people disturb nests. Tommy doesn't do well with reasons and ignores me. I aim a kick at him from across the tree-trunk and he loses his balance.

"Fuck off!" he yells, grabbing for the trunk with both hands. The chick falls to the ground.

I clamber down and pick up the tiny creature. "It's dead," I say, cradling it in my hand. It looks like it's sleeping, and it's warm, too.

"It's all your fault for kicking me," Tommy says, climbing down behind me. "Maybe it's stunned, or disoriented?" I say.

He reaches for it, but I won't let him have it. Instead, I put it in the pocket of my pants and run down the lane to where Mam waits at the front door.

"Get in out of that. I'll have your tea on the table in a jiffy," she says.

In the kitchen, cigarette butts stick out of the dead potted plant on the window ledge. The smell goes up my nostrils and makes me queasy. Mam smokes forty a day and her fingers are orange like carrots.

Mam's belly doesn't look much bigger and I try to picture the baby inside her like the bird in the egg from the tree. What if humans laid eggs and sat on them instead of having the baby grow inside? That'd make Mam's life a bit easier, and she'd not be suffering from her bunions because of the extra weight. I worry that the baby will turn out orange too from all the cigarette smoke Mam inhales. I don't want an orange-skinned brother or sister. I want a nice little pink bundle of joy like the nurse at school says Mam will have soon enough.

The doorbell rings as Mam is putting my tea on the

table, and it's the life insurance man. She tells him that we're strapped for cash this week. The Old Man is in the North Sea and won't be back until the end of the month. He scribbles in his notebook with a pencil and after she signs the book he tells her he'll take the payment next time. When the door shuts she says that she's weary and has her fingers worked to the bone. I disappear into the sitting room and read *Oliver Twist* by the fireplace.

We have sardine sandwiches and mashed potatoes for tea, and she says Grace, the cutlery and napkin in the Old Man's place, waiting for his return from sea. Small bites are what I take, chewing each one thirty-three times, exactly as Uncle Harry says when we visit his house. I'm not allowed to put my elbows on the table, and I'm not allowed to speak. Uncle Harry says little boys should be seen and not heard.

"That's not reasonable," Mam said to the Old Man once, when Uncle Harry went outside for a minute, but he gave her a vicious look and that was that.

The dead bird is safe and I spread salad cream on my sardines to take away the fishy taste. I bet the chick would have liked a sardine from me, instead of death.

"What have you boys been up to?" Mam asks.

"Nothing." I mumble through a mouthful of toast and sardines, the oiliness weird on my tongue. I'm blushing. I know I am. When I tell a lie, my face reddens. Mam says I'm just like the Old Man when it comes to deception.

She clicks at me and takes a sup of her tea. Maybe the chick's mother is back at the nest with a worm for it to eat? I bet the mother bird loved her child. The Old Man says that one of the keys to happiness is love. The sardines and toast choke me, and the dead chick grows cold inside my pants' pocket.

I'm shunting my peas to one side of my plate, scientifically, making sure I do it in groups of three, when she taps her glass with the fork.

"Stop playing with your food," she says.

All I wanted to do was make a maze out of the mashed potatoes, but I say nothing. Her glass is Waterford, the last one left. The others broke when the shelf in the bureau crashed to the ground last year. She was in floods of tears for the entire day, because the crystal was from her grandmother. "What's done is done, and can't be undone," she said at the time. The Old Man hugged her that day, and he kept repeating words I couldn't hear. I hope she never breaks this one, because if she does I don't know what she'll do.

She traces patterns in the flour she sifts for baking bread on Mondays: intricate floral spirals, dancers on cold snow. We're sitting by the kitchen fireplace, when the far-off sound of an airplane overhead rattles the windows and sets the neighborhood cats to mewling. She curses at the five tabbies clumped together on the roof of the neighbor's garage, all discordant and orange. I grin, watching my spit bubble and steam on the hot coals as she kneads the dough.

Our floor shines in the harsh light from the bare bulb over the kitchen door. We used to have more light, but the fluorescent strip broke last month and we are waiting for the Old Man to fix it. Still, I like how the harsh light plays tricks with me, sometimes causing me to see his face outside in the coal shed when in fact he is hundreds of miles away at sea.

When tea is over Mam buttons her coat, and slips on her shiny high-heeled shoes, the ones she wears to Mass on high days and holidays.

"I'm going to the corner shop," she says, pausing at the hall mirror to put lipstick on. Her lacquered nails shine in the hallway, the baby safe inside her, and the same pierced shade of crimson on her lips. She looks back and waves, her mouth a garish wound of cherry.

The tickle in my throat stops me from saying anything else, and as she quits the house I watch her shadow through the panes of the front door. I make it into the front room as she steps off the curb and into the falling mist.

Chapter 10

The Old Man says we'll be off on our holliers to the West of Ireland in a few weeks. He's booked a cottage by the edge of the Atlantic Ocean in County Mayo near the village of Mulrany, and it's near a golf course, so he's promised to take me out for a few rounds if I behave myself between now and then. He says it's going to be a breath of fresh air.

We spend the first Saturday he's home cleaning the gutters and getting the window frames ready to paint. He likes to do these jobs because he says the workmen around here are all botch mechanics and can't paint a bloody thing.

On Sunday, the phone rings at six in the morning. The Old Man's soothing voice suggest something bad has happened. Mam knocks on the door a few minutes later and comes into my room. "Your grandmother is dead," she says, tears falling. "Say a prayer for her with me."

We kneel. "For the repose of her soul." That's all, no more, no less. She sits at the foot of the bed and sobs. I am mute. No words; no comfort. I have no experience with death. She tells me to put some clothes in a bag because the funeral is in two days and we'll leave this afternoon for Athleague.

We drive off before noon, through pastureland dotted with sheep, towns built around tall steeples, and rivers cold-flowing to the sea. I play I-spy with myself watching out for something beginning with K. On the outskirts of Tuam we pass a group of travelers at a campsite; their caravans all greens, yellows, and reds, and small shuttered doors at the backs of them.

"Fecking foreigners," the Old Man says. "Hungarians, or Romanians, stealing children and worse."

They're silent in the front of the Wolseley, until we drive through our old hometown. The Old Man cranks the window down and spits phlegm towards the Bank of Ireland on the corner of Main Street. Customers on the curb stare at him and shake their heads.

"The devil take them and their thieving ways," is all he says.

Mam grips his hand and says, "Let it go, for goodness sake. It's all in the past."

"By God, they robbed me blind. Didn't they take the wallet from my pocket and turn us out in the street," he says. "That's some bloody rigmarole."

"Ah, we're better off now. You're a changed man since you went to work on the oilrigs," she says, squeezing his hand.

We stop at a tea house in Athleague before going on to Uncle Harry's for the wake.

A waitress swishes by and the Old Man winks. Mam wrinkles her nose.

"A thing of beauty is a joy forever," he says.

Mam shoots him a mean look.

"My hero," she says.

She stirs her coffee over and over, keeping an eye on the waitress.

The Old Man snorts and I know he wants something stronger, but Mam has warned him there's to be no drinking before the funeral.

The music is loud, Thin Lizzy singing "The Boys are Back in Town."

"Would you turn down that jungle music?" he asks.

The manager standing behind the counter raises an eyebrow and speaks to the waitress. She's not happy and says something I can't hear.

"Well," he says, plugging his pipe with tobacco and striking a match, "we'd better head off and bury the old hoor, now."

"God forgive you," Mam says, and rattles her coffee cup on the saucer. I count the eyeholes in the front of my shoes over and over again.

The Old Man parks outside Uncle Harry's place and we enter through the side-door. Auntie Martha hugs each of us in turn and bustles about making tea. According to Uncle Harry, Granny breathed her last sometime about nine o'clock. Uncle Harry scrubs away with a toothbrush, singing "The Old Triangle," at the top of his lungs.

The Old Man laughs at this and musses my hair. "Your uncle is a great man for the songs," he explains. "I remember when he joined the British army in World War II, he was thrown out for singing about rebellion and the Easter Rising."

Mam cries and cries, and says, "I wish she could have lived to see the new baby." The Old Man wraps her in his arms and kisses her head.

Mam and Auntie Martha scrub the kitchen table, the Vim in Mam's rubber-gloved hand, her other holding a wire wool pad, the usual cigarette between her lips. She says nothing when she sees the mess of plates and rotten food in the kitchen.

"What in the name of God has happened, Martha?" Mam asks.

Auntie Martha sits on a chair and sobs. She tells Mam

about her nerves and how she can't manage at all, and how Harry is away gallivanting about with the bank manager playing golf all over the countryside.

Mam's face puckers, as if cleaning up the mess is the last thing she wants to do in the world. She gets up from the floor where she's been kneeling and grimaces. A book is on the chair in the kitchen, and the spine had the name "Tennyson," in embossed gilt letters.

"What's this one?" I ask.

She inhales, the cigarette flaming up, and expels two streams of smoke out her nose. She recites, "Oh, 'The splendor falls on castle walls and snowy summits old in story: the long light shakes across the lakes, and the wild cataract leaps in glory.'"

The Old Man squeezes her waist, and he continues, "'Blow, bugle, blow, set the wild echoes flying, blow bugle; answer, echoes,'" and Mam joins in with, "'Dying, dying, dying.'"

In the dim kitchen of the house it's as if I'm in a dream where my parents are happy together, and the sound of Tennyson has made it so. Maybe I'll be allowed to take the book home to Dublin with me after the funeral.

Granny is laid out for the wake in the front room, the coffin resting on ta trestle table, the lid propped open by the window. I've never seen a dead person before. The dried-out corpse, the rosary beads entwined in her right fist and the picture of Saint Thérèse of Lisieux in her other hand.

The visitors come and go all afternoon and into the early evening. When the last one finally leaves the house, Uncle Harry latches the door and says, "Thank Jesus that's over."

Mam and the Old Man visit with Uncle Harry and Auntie Martha, and I walk outside to the back yard where the brambles are thick and wild in the garden and an old rusted lawnmower sits beside a small table with a half-empty bottle of Club Orange. I can see the pulp in the bottom of the bottle and wonder if it was Granny's last drink.

From over the wall the sound of a transistor radio plays ELO's, "Can't Get it Out of My Head," and as I wave my arms about and sing to myself I might be inviting the Old Man's ridicule if he looks out the window and sees me. I take a lint-covered Kola Cube out of my pocket and suck it in the garden; the radio changes to Neil Sedaka's, "O Carol." A wasp buzzes about my head and I flick at it with my hand, wondering if Granny died in her sleep, or was awake at the moment of death.

I toss and turn in bed as the moon tumbles through the open curtains and casts crooked shadow limbs on the wall from the tree outside. The shadow is the bent outline of a crone, and resembles the old lady from number twelve who died a few years ago. Flit of owl's wings on the wall makes it look as if she's going to grab me by the neck. Do I yell out in the dark and waken the house, or do I cringe beneath the tucked sheets and wiggle my toes inside the hot water bottle cover for courage?

I suffer the wetness of the bed when the pee comes. I don't want the Old Man to think I'm a "namby-pamby *gossoon*." He'll nickname me "piss the bed," and tell Mam I should wash my own bloody bed sheets. I overheard her once with Mrs. O'Malley, talking about my bedwetting and she whispered the words, "delicate lad."

I take the wet pajama pants off and creep into the corner beside the dresser. What am I going to do for the rest of the night as the tree shadows climb the wall and the crone appears again? I hear the Old Man's voice mocking me as I huddle naked against the wall. I bundle the sheets up in a ball and sleep under the bed.

In the morning, we get ready to drive out to Athleague Cemetery. All I hear are mumbled voices and old men doffing their caps. The procession winds its way through the town, past the shops and buildings of Mam's childhood. The black serpentine of people follows the patent-polished hearse, the brassbound coffin inside the glass-paneled vehicle. The Old Man, his arm around Mam's shoulders, props her up as she goes toward the family plot. The black lace of her headscarf flutters in the breeze. Clouds, grey-filled and rain-laden, scud across the sky.

At the graveyard, the headstones are shrouded by oak and elm; the heavy branches hang over the ancient crosses and angels. Several people kneel by graves on the Protestant side of the graveyard, and on the Catholic side, a large crowd congregates at Granny's grave.

The brass-handled coffin rests on beams and fists drop clay on its pine-shined lid. Uncle Harry stands to one side shaking hands with the mourners. The Old Man grips my uncle's hand and whispers something in his ear. Whatever passes between them goes unheard.

Uncle Harry stands with Auntie Martha and watches the Old Man stomp off to the car. I follow, looking over my shoulder at my uncle's crow-black figure pressing flesh. What sort of people are my relatives? What's going on with Aunt Martha's nervous condition, and Uncle Harry's house loan to the Old Man, and what did Uncle Harry say to him at the side of the grave?

Two weeks later, I return to the big abandoned Edwardian house next-door to Lahart's Garage. The corrugated iron over the front door is filled with graffiti and torn posters advertising Fossett's Circus and Christmas pantomimes from years gone by. The overgrown front garden is full of the whiff of spilled motor oil and rubber tires.

Long shadows from the horse-chestnut tree in the front yard trail up the red-bricked walls. Virginia creeper crawls all the way to the eaves, where a sparrow bobs in and out of a wood-knot, almost hidden by the ivy.

At the side of the house, rickety ladders and ancient paint buckets, covered in the same blue-royal dribbles as the eaves. I hug the wall as if at any moment the entire house is about to devour me. As I sidle along by the rear of the building, beads of sweat collect on my forehead. A tight fist squeezes my walnut-sized heart.

Swallowing hard, I glance through the window to the left of the front door. A giant hole in the floor exposes the basement some twenty feet below, a few planks of flooring and ceiling fragments jutting out from the walls.

In the web-strewn corner of the room, deep in the dark, elevated four feet above the wrecked floorboards, my grandmother floats, her white hair shining in the darkness, a crooked finger beckoning me. Something gives way and my pants dampen. I sprint home as fast as I can, run up the stairs, into the toilet, bolt the door and slump to the floor.

I keep the secret of Granny's ghost in a small, painted box, wrapped in cotton wool. She is a floating secret, light as red feathers, heavy as the thump of a dead tree-limb falling on drifted snow. A cry wells from my larynx, and my Adam's apple bobs with a steady rhythm. On the corrugated shed roof, a white seabird stands silently on one leg—one skinny limb supporting its body's weight—the bird's crest waving in the breeze.

I let go of the sound—the kept vowels and consonants of grief, watch them escape into the air, like a caged creature given an open window. My wail goes out into the world, rips through the air and fills the brimless vessel of the day.

The sadness I've felt since Granny's death has been difficult. Mam is distracted with the new baby and I'm left to my own devices most of the time. Right now, from the sitting room window the smoking chimney of the Hellfire Club on top of the Dublin Mountains are visible. Magpies like a shattered chessboard mosaic chatter in the neighbor's monkey puzzle tree.

116

Mam is in the kitchen making brown bread, the serrated knife cutting a cross into wet dough. The rasp of a striking match interrupts my reading and cigarette ash festoons the unbaked loaf. The sun falls. Across the road, a small child pulls a pot of boiling water off a stove. I take out the *Collected Poems of Robert Frost* from the bookcase in the dining room and transport myself to a New England landscape where birch trees sway in the breeze.

The print on the page is blurry and I can't keep my eyes open. Finally, I kiss Mam goodnight and climb the stairs to bed. The landing floorboards creak and groan for no apparent reason. I convince myself these shivering adjustments in the architecture are more than ancient, creaking timbers. They are my dead Granny's footfalls. I know if I go out to the landing she'll be there, a fluttering apparition in the darkness waiting to drag me into the cobwebbed attic with skeletal hands.

Mam sits downstairs, cup of tea in hand, the television blaring and her cigarette filling the air with wreaths of smoke. Her stomach is bigger now, the baby growing every day. I'm still not able to leave the bedroom at night for fear of the ghosts. I get out of bed and feel my way to the window in the darkness. A dim crack of light from the neighbor's house shines through a hole in the curtains. I undo my pajama pants and slow, slow, slow, let the pee run down the wallpaper onto the champagne-colored carpet. Back to bed, and I'm ashamed at not being able to go down the hall to the bathroom like a normal boy.

Barry and Gerry Golden, the twins, are exceptional footballers, and whenever we choose teams for five-a-side soccer they're the automatically chosen captains and pick from the rest of us for sides.

The lane we play in is opposite our front garden and in

full view of Dempsey's front door and windows. The strip of tarmacadam is about ten feet wide and thirty yards long. At either end we mark goalposts with bundled up sweaters. Because of the narrowness, the game usually gets bogged down in no-man's land with all of us hacking at the ball through a thicket of legs.

Barry's first shot sails above my head, takes one bounce and slams into the Dempsey's front door.

Barry screams, "Gooooolllllll!!!"

"Aw shut up, ya spa, your shot was over the bar," Gerry shouts.

Next thing they're face to face and the air is wet with saliva as they argue over the goal. Barry walks over the road and opens the gate to the Dempsey's garden. He marches straight to the ball, but before he can get it, the door flies open and a furious Dempsey bellows, "Get out of my garden!"

"Give us the bleeding ball back, mister," Barry says.

Dempsey looks him up and down and disappears into the house. Barry just stands there at the door and repeatedly chants, "Give us the bleeding ball back, you tosser!"

Next thing the door opens again and Dempsey's there, a garden rake grasped in both hands. He pokes it at Barry's chest and nudges him towards the gate.

"Get out! Get out! Get out of my garden, you cur!" He jabs the rake repeatedly Barry's chest.

"No! Not 'til we get our ball back," Barry roars.

At this point my mother is at our door and asks Barry to go home before Mr. Dempsey has a heart attack.

Barry stands there, unrelenting, and says, "We're not going until I get the ball back from that old bollocks."

He chucks a stone full force at Dempsey's door, and it lifts a chunk of paint from the doorframe. Our purple-face neighbor appears and screeches at Barry, "I've summoned the guards now, so I have. I'm an Easter Rising survivor, you know? And don't try to run away, I know where you live."

"Go fuck yourself, you old bollocks," Barry retorts, giving him two fingers and throwing the ball at the old man's head.

Dempsey punctures the ball with the rake, reaches across the gate and swings the deflated plastic in a wide arc. The ball catches Barry smack on the side of the cheek, a loose flap of plastic whips across his face and opens an ugly red gash. Barry puts a hand to his cheek and takes it away again to see blood on his fingers.

"You cut me! Jaysus!" Barry shouts, going after him.

Mrs. Dempsey waits at the door. "Bill! Bill! Come in out of that. Leave the young thug alone," she says. "Let the guards deal with him now."

Barry has his hands on the lapels of the old fellow's jacket. He shakes him, the blood flying in a fine spray from his cheek. Barry pushes him hard, and Dempsey goes down on the flowerbed, crushing his wife's carnations, his hat falling on the path. Barry lashes a boot at the fallen man and yells, "Look at you now! Easter Rising me arse. You're a fecking joke." He turns around, leaves the garden, and walks back to the rest of us who stare at him open-mouthed.

A couple of days before we're to leave for our holiday, the Old Man runs his thick hand across my scalp and ruffles my fair hair. He declares, "You need a haircut—a good feckin' skelping. Yourself and your pals are lost the run of yourselves. After what you did to Mr. Dempsey, next door, I think drastic measures are necessary."

The white-and-red striped pole of the barbershop swirls in the distance like a severed limb swathed in bandages. There's the one haircut on the chalkboard outside McKeown & Sons: Men's Haircut - £3.00.

The clanging of the bell startles the Skinner from his newspaper.

"Well now! Well now! Mr. Brogan, what's it to be then?"

he says, rubbing sandpaper hands together. "Yourself and the lad, is it?"

I sneak a bit closer to the Old Man.

"Just the lad today, Mr. McKeown," he says. "Give him a good skelping. He's like a bloody Nancy Boy."

"£1, then for the young fella," McKeown says to the Old Man.

The executioner's chair is bolted to the floor. The Skinner fastens a smock over my head and cinches a grimy towel about my neck. He snips the scissors in his one hand and dusts my shoulders with a brush in the other. A black comb from a jar of electric blue Barbasol appears. The Skinner parts my hair as church bells ring out.

"Weren't you in class with our Willie?" the Skinner asks. "He does be telling me all about you. Yiz must be thrilled skinny to be on your holliers."

"Yes. Grand, thanks!" I reply. "Don't take off too much, please."

My hair floats to the linoleum floor as the scissors snick away in his fingers.

The Old Man is knee-deep in the obituary column of the *Irish Independent*. He won't budge even if the winner of the 2:30 at Punchestown Racetrack gallops through the place. The Skinner's goop-filled eyes stare back at me from the mirror as he feels his way about my scalp with his fingers.

I grab my ear. My fingers are bloody. The Skinner grabs a towel and dabs at my head in apology. He blames his fading eyesight. I feel like a fool on the walk home, the thick wad of Mercurochrome-stained cotton wool taped to my ear.

When we get home the Old Man says it's still too long and makes me sit on the kitchen stool, a towel around my shoulders and his beer breath warming my neck. He plunks a Tupperware bowl on my head and goes around it with the clippers. When I see the damage in the bathroom mirror I wish I were back at the Skinner's. I look like one of those monks bent over the desk, working on the *Book of Kells*.

The day before we leave, I'm steaming stamps off envelopes for my stamp collection and Mam is wrapping cups and saucers in brown paper for the rental cottage. The Old Man is up the road at a session in Coman's and won't be home until closing time. Mam's nylons are on the clotheshorse by the range in the kitchen and she's got all our underwear in a basket ready to iron.

It's my job to make sure Tommy takes care of DeValera while we're away. He's going to take her for a walk and make sure she's fed and watered every day for the fortnight. Mam and Dad arranged it with Tommy's parents, and the Old Man said he'd slip Tommy a tenner for looking after the dog.

I'm bringing *Treasure Island, The Lost World,* and *The RSPB Book of Birds* with me for the fortnight. If I'm lucky I'll be allowed to buy some books when we're on the other side of the country, and maybe I can discover some rare bird that never lands on our shores while I'm at it.

My school jotter will be the place I keep track of the birds I see. After I tear out the mathematics problems and the doodles from class the notebook is clean and ready for the holidays. I write "PATRICK BROGAN: BIRDWATCHER & EXPLORER," on the cover in orange marker. I put everything in a suitcase with tartan lining, and place my clothes on top, the coin purse at the bottom folded in a neat square made from my treasure map.

I stay awake listening for magic in the night. The Old Man's key rattles in the latch and his footsteps thump on the stairs as he comes to bed. Maybe on holliers we'll do stuff together. He never has time for me because he works so hard. Still, I love him because that's what you're meant to do for your parents—love them. Sometimes it's difficult, but as Father McDaid says, Jesus is love.

Mam tells Mrs. Golden how the Old Man begged, borrowed, and stole so he could take off three weeks, giving us time to drive out and time for him to rest before returning to the rig.

We stop at Jack's roadhouse so the Old Man can wet his whistle. Mam sips at a glass of Seven-Up with a cherry floating in the ice, and he says, "Ah, that's grand," after taking a long mouthful of Guinness. A creamy mustache foams his upper lip. His whiskey sits untouched on the counter.

I suck my Club Orange through a straw and two boys play Space Invaders in the corner, the green spacemen dropping down the screen in a hurry. One of the boys punches the other in the arm, and says, "Move over, I'm an expert."

Mam says, "It's a relief to stop for a while," and the Old Man shakes his head in agreement. Her belly is round like a football and I hope the seat belt doesn't harm the baby. What if it pinched the baby's head, or cut off its blood supply? The bubbles I'm blowing in the orange spray stuff onto my shirt and the Old Man clenches a fist and brings it down on the counter.

"Sorry, Da," I say.

"By God, we raised you better than that," he says.

I finger the straw and Mam winces, a little moan escaping her lips.

"Is it the baby?" the Old Man asks, placing a meaty hand on her stomach.

"Ah, it's kicking a little bit," she says.

"Can I feel it? Can I?" I ask.

The Old Man says, "Leave your mother alone."

"God, now isn't he only curious," she says, and takes my hand. "Good lad," she whispers, and puts it on her tummy, where after a while something shifts. I pull my hand away.

"Would you prefer a little brother, or a sister?" she asks me.

"I hope it's a boy, so we can climb trees and play soccer,"

I reply.

She undoes her cardigan and rubs the bump as the Old Man holds a glass of whiskey to the light.

We get back to the car and the Old Man helps Mam slide into her seat, because now she's so big she can barely fit.

We're in heavy traffic heading west when a big van rushes by us, almost causing the Old Man to go off the road.

"Ignorant bostoon," he yells.

I keep my nose stuck in *Treasure Island* and say nothing.

"Calm down, Ronan," Mam says, her hand on his knee. He puts his hand on hers and tells her not to worry, and accelerates after the van. The liquor from Jack's Roadhouse is dangerous and when he zips by three cars and almost goes into the ditch trying to avoid an oncoming funeral, Mam runs out of patience.

"Are you trying to kill us all? Jesus, Ronan, I know you don't want another mouth to feed, but this is ridiculous."

"Shut your trap." He presses his foot on the accelerator with purpose. She tenses in her seat and blesses herself to stave off our deaths. Meanwhile, I'm setting sail on the Hispaniola with Captain Silver and the crew running their flags up the mizzenmast.

Mam lights a cigarette and the car fills with smoke. She opens the ashtray in the middle of the dashboard and lipstick-stained butts stick out like tombstones. Her hand sweeps the ash from her lap and the Old Man drives on, the dotted lines in the middle of the road disappearing faster than the space invaders in the pub.

St. Christopher holds the baby tight on the medal that hangs from the rear-view mirror, afraid we'll crash, I'm certain. The swaying of the medal makes it appear as if the saint is alive and rocking the baby from side to side in a slow waltz.

We catch up with the van and the Old Man keeps the horn pressed for a long time as we overtake it. He gives the driver the two fingers and Mam says, "God forgive you, Ronan."

The Old Man says nothing, his energy focused on the road ahead and the next opportunity to wet his whistle.

The cigarette-scented car is a prison and even though I pretend I'm a pirate on the Hispaniola, I know there's no escape. Slowly, I open the wrapper of a Macaroon bar and remove the chocolate bit by bit with my teeth. In front of us the sinking sun disappears behind the nearing mountains and Mam crushes another cigarette butt in the ashtray, grinding it into the other gravestones. I wish I was lucky enough to be a Jim Hawkins, a ship's boy away at sea, sort of like the Old Man; though the oilrigs stay in the same place all the time.

We finally pull up outside the cottage that'll be our home for the fortnight. It's dark and an owl hoots from a nearby tree. Across the road, a dog growls from behind a wire gate, and the Old Man shouts at me to help carry stuff inside.

"I hope they control that bloody dog," he mutters.

The cottage is dark and the corners of the big living room are spiderwebbed and shadowed. The ceiling is low and I can reach the beams with my hands.

"Sure, this is grand," the Old Man says, putting a suitcase on the ground with a thump.

The roof rack is filled with the rest of our suitcases and while Mam finds her way to the kitchen to start cooking our tea, we unload everything. As I'm going out the door the Old Man trips on a shoe scraper and stumbles. I put my arms out to stop him from falling and as he regains his balance, the sour smell of beer and whiskey hits me in the face.

"Jesus Christ, who put that bloody thing there?" he asks, aiming a kick at it and cursing again.

I cringe when he tries to kick it again. "Sorry. I was trying to help," I say.

"Ah, don't mind me. I'm getting old," he says, fastening his coat and bringing in the last suitcase.

Away over the sea the moon is a glazed orange ball. A harvest moon. "Look at the moon," I say.

When Mam comes out and we stand looking into the sky, even the Old Man admits it's a beautiful night. "The glory of God," he says, a grin on his face for once.

"Will you come in for your tea?" Mam asks, wiping her hands on the apron. "The sausages will only be good for dog food if you don't eat them soon."

"The lad and I are going to look up at the stars for a while," he says, putting his arm around my shoulder.

We stay outside for a good half-hour as he points out the constellations.

"Do you see Orion, there?" he asks. "There's the belt that goes with it. Orion is the hunter, you know?"

This is as close as I've ever felt to him and I say a silent prayer for it to always be this good.

"I used to call you Hunter, when you were just a wee lad."

"Why don't you use that name anymore?" I ask.

"Arrah, you're big now. Almost a man. No need for nicknames at your age."

Inside, the luggage is put away and the cottage smells of rashers and sausages. Mam has the fire going, turf briquettes blaze in the hearth and the radio plays the evening Mart & Market report. Heifers are at a record price, and Leo Yellow Injectors are just the thing for mastitis, according to the farmer reading the report.

We sit down to tea and the Old Man licks his lips, the plate in front of him piled high with rashers, sausages, fried tomatoes, and toast. "Bless us Our Lord, and these thy gifts," he begins.

"Which of thy bounty, we are about to receive," I say.

"Through Christ, Our Lord," he adds.

"Amen." The three of us make the sign of the cross and the clicking of knives and forks on plates commences.

Mam picks at her food, wincing now and then from the baby's kicks. "Don't worry, I'm grand. It's a touch of indigestion," she says, pushing a half-eaten sausage around her plate.

I know she doesn't want the baby to detract from our holidays, but she can't help it. The Old Man reaches across and helps himself to what's left on her plate. A slice of bacon falls on his lap and stains his pants. "Shite," he says, picking the rasher off the floor and forking it into his mouth.

After tea, I wander down to the wall at the end of the field. It's made of rough stones, all laid on top of each other without any cement. Spongy green and yellow mosses and lichen cover many of the stones, and overhead, a galaxy of stars spreads out against the heavens. I imagine the Apollo rocket making its way to the moon, Aldrin, Armstrong, and Michael Collins heading for the lunar surface.

For a long time, I believed he was the same Michael Collins we read about in Irish History at school, but the teacher smacked me on the head and told me not to be thick, and he was sure there were no rockets going to the moon at the Easter Rising, only the souls of the departed patriots whose names we learned by heart in school.

In the gloaming, I recite their names into the holy night. Whispering to the stars, I name each separate star after one of them: "Pádraig Pearse, Thomas McDonagh, Thomas Clarke, Joseph Mary Plunkett, William Pearse, Edward Daly, Michael O'Hanrahan, John McBride, Éamonn Ceannt, Michael Mallin, Seán Heuston, Con Colbert, James Connolly, and Sean MacDiarmada." When I finish, a single star fizzes across the sky and I'm not sure, but it's probably the ghost of my favorite patriot Con Colbert, who was executed in the Stonebreaker's Yard at Kilmainham Gaol on the 5th of May 1916.

As the moon spins above me the sound of the Old Man singing "Boulavogue," in the kitchen floats across the meadow. Mam's voice joins in. "For Father Murphy of the County Wexford Sweeps o'er the land like a mighty wave." Over the water a fog rolls in from the Atlantic and something rustles at the bottom of the field.

Inside they're drinking whiskey by the fire and talking about ancient family history. The Old Man shouts, "Shite. I was in my prime, and we left that place like thieves in the night." There's no sound from Mam and I know she's tired because of the baby.

Mam and the Old Man have the larger bedroom and I've got the little room at the back where the roof slopes down to meet the wall. In the dusty thatch, there are spiders and I hope they don't fall on me in the night. I tent the covers and switch on my torch to read *Treasure Island* in the dark.

Turning the pages in torchlight is my favorite thing to do on holidays, and when the light flickers I switch off the torch to conserve the battery. I unscrew the back of the torch to check the power and my tongue fizzes from the battery acid.

I hope we get to go play golf as the Old Man promised. He's got his Ben Hogan clubs with him, and his ancient mashie niblick. He says it belonged to Old Tom Morris, but when I ask who that is, he shakes his head and says, "Never mind, sure what are they teaching you at all?"

The ocean crashes onto the shore at the bottom of the field, and I wish I could row out into the sea and search for islands where there might be buried treasure. I've never rowed a boat, but I want to learn. Maybe the Old Man will enquire in town whether there are any people nearby who could give me lessons.

As the moon shines bright, the waves thunder, my eyes close and dreams come. Tomorrow, I shall explore the ruined cottages up the road and see if I can find any treasure left behind by the dead.

Chapter 11

Mam, at the stove, makes breakfast, and the Old Man wears shorts that show his knobbly knees. He has purple wormlike veins on his legs and wingtip shoes paired with Argyll socks. He hates foreign holidays and remarks about the purity and beauty of Ireland's coastline. "Sure, what business would we have to travel to Brighton or Blackpool or the South of France for that matter? They're third-rate towns with bad food and ignorant heathens. You get a better class of person in the Irish countryside."

Mam nods in agreement, and fills his plate with rashers, sausages and eggs. The Old Man goes at the fry up, knife and fork working overtime. He mops the grease up with a slice of fried bread and slurps his cup of tea down. Mam eats her own breakfast in-between washing and drying the frying pan and dishes from last night's dinner. I go to help her but she waves me off with a swish of the tea-towel.

After eating my fry I'm off to find a good spot to bury the treasure I brought from the house. The weight of the chain link purse in my pocket makes me nervous and I'm praying the coins don't jangle and give me away.

"Good lad," he says, when he sees me about to head out the door. "Watch out for wild creatures hiding in the gorse."

"Ah, Ronan, don't scare the boy with your nonsense," Mam says, kissing me on the head. "Run along now and enjoy yourself. I'm going to take a little rest."

The morning sun shatters the brilliant blue of the Atlantic Ocean. Two rabbits bounce across the field, white tails darting in and out of the long grass. At the bottom of the field a stream flows cold down to the estuary where I'll go bird watching with my *RSPB Book of Birds* and the Old Man's Zeiss binoculars.

I take the scrap of parchment with the map on it, and mark the distance from the low wall to a crooked tree that hangs over the river. Twenty paces west, fifteen paces north, and twelve paces east. I remove the treasure from my pants and dig away the earth around the base of the tree. When the hole is deep enough, I put the package into it and cover it up with dirt. I scratch out a rough skull and crossbones on a large rock and turn it upside down so nobody knows it's there except me. When we return next year, I can unearth the treasure and take it back to Dublin.

A rusted gate that leads to the water's edge is chained shut, so I clamber over it. A skull rests in the weeds, buried in a clump of buttercups. The white bone is covered with greenish moss and the loose teeth rattle about, insecure in their sockets. When I run my fingers over the teeth they're dull and pitted in places. Some of the skull is damaged and shards of bone stick out, and I'm sure it'd make a great weapon if a mad bull with big horns attacked me. Maybe it belongs to a badger or a fox, or even a sheep?

I hop onto a rock in the middle of the narrow stream and hold the skull up to the sky. "Alas, poor Yorick. I knew him well…" I recite the Bard and know I must look like an awful eejit. Above me, the evening star is visible in the windless sky, and one cloud hangs silent in the faded blue. Back through the field I travel, all business, the skull secured in the crook of my arm like a rugby ball.

We leave our shoes outside the cottage because Mam says she doesn't want sand on the floor. The mist rolls in off the Atlantic and flowers the area in gray moisture. The Old Man pulls me aside and opens the window. "Can you hear the voices?" he says.

We listen, but only the crawk of a seagull comes out of the fine rain.

"There are lost souls out there," the Old Man says. His two arms are wrapped about me and the warm smell of Old Spice is everywhere. "Lasses from the village who lost their lovers to the sea," he goes on.

I don't say a word, listening closer for the cries of the dead. Away down the field the waves murmur, the pining cries of those who died of broken hearts. The Old Man sucks the stem of his pipe and strikes a match against the whitewashed cottage wall. Soon, we are engulfed in a cloud of Erinmore, and in the smoke, he sings a Clancy Brother's song. "And the ocean waves do roll, and the stormy winds do blow, and we poor sailors are skipping at the top, while the landlubbers lie down below, below, below, while the landlubbers lie down below."

We stay in the same place for the longest time, the mist thickening and the afternoon still so many hours away. "You know you're a good *gossoon*," he says.

My throat tightens and I shut my eyes tight. "I love you." The words catch in my throat as I whisper them.

"Will we play golf tomorrow, Da?"

"Son, we will take the clubs and the caddy cart and strike out for the links in the morning," he replies.

True to his word, the next day after breakfast we drive the bumpy path to the pre-fab clubhouse and check-in with the old fellow who sits supping a mug of tea. The Old Man takes a handful of colored tees and a scorecard and we get back in the car and drive over the course to the edge of the ocean where the 9th tee awaits.

He plants a ball on an orange tee and sticks it in the ground. He wiggles his backside twice and moves the club head back and forth. "Slow and easy. Keep your eye on the ball," he says. "A cool head, and a tight hole is the secret to this life."

He strikes the small white ball and sends it sailing into the stratosphere. His stroke is beautiful and I wish he would teach me how. When I tee the ball up and take a few practice swings, he tells me to slow it down. I swing again, fast and wild, my head lifting, and the ball rolls off the tee and trickles a few feet backwards. The Old Man laughs and re-tees the ball for me.

"Keep your head down. It's all in the hips. Swing from the hips," he says, grabbing me by the waist and pivoting me around.

I swing again, this time connecting with the ball, but it scutters along the grass. The clean white ball nestles in a big cowpat. "Hurrah for shite," he shouts, clapping me on the back.

Up dunes and into dried-up cart tracks we go. When he hits the ball there's a lovely fizz to it and it arrows straight and true towards the far-off green. When I hit the ball nothing good happens. I get frustrated and the Old Man laughs even more.

By the end of the eighteen holes I've half-a-mind to swing the one wood and catch him between the eyes. Instead, I pull the caddy cart along behind me and swear I'll never pester him to play golf ever again.

We stop at the village bar in Mulrany, and he stands me a

lemonade and chats with the barmaid about all sorts of tripe. By the time we get back to the cottage, Mam is banging pans about and frying up the dinner. She asks if I had a nice time, and all I can do is lie.

The baby is growing and Mam's belly is enormous. I feel bad for her having to carry around all that weight. She did all of this with me fifteen years ago. That's seems like a lot of distance between babies. Most of my friends' brothers and sisters are a few years apart. Still, I know she's happy about the baby, because she's collecting knitting patterns for the clothes she's going to make.

I sit in the small chair by the fire, next to the peat briquettes, and the flames flicker and flash redbluegreen in the fireplace. Outside the sky is darkening and drops of rain pitter against the window. A storm is coming in and the animals and birds must be seeking shelter. How did the ancient monks in their small stone oratories survive so many storms over their lifetimes?

I delve into my *Pears Encyclopedia* and read some facts about the prayer schedule at monasteries. The names are Latin, and we learnt their meaning in class. *Vigil, Lauds, Matins, Vespers, Eucharist.* I don't want to be a monk, though. They live austere lives and can't get married. But that might be a good thing given how Mam and the Old Man are always going at each other, like a pair of fighting hens.

I know Tommy's parents fight, too, and he's told me about the one time his da threw the iron at the wall because his ma wouldn't iron his shirts properly. Why do people get married if all they're going to do is hurt each other? I wonder whether I'm going to meet someone who'll marry me one day? Maybe Cathy and I will get "hitched" as John Wayne says in *The Searchers*. I won't be the sort of a husband the Old Man is to Mam. I promise myself, as the fire warms my legs, that I'll treat my wife with love and respect no matter how mad she makes me.

It would be great to have x-ray vision, and be able to not just see through objects, but also to see into the future. If I could see into my future I'd know the sex of the baby, and who is going to win the next World Cup in Argentina. I could go on the Late Late Show with Gay Byrne and shock Mam and the Old Man with my powers.

Two weeks by the sea in the thatched cottage and Mam is weary from late nights with the Old Man in the local pub, and making breakfast, dinner, and tea every day. As she says, "Your Da can't boil an egg. Sure, am I not raising two boys in this house?" She repeats this over and over during our time in Mulrany, but when I ask if I can help, she shoos me and tells me to get out from under her feet.

Mam has no appetite and goes to lie down, and the Old Man has a stern look on his face, the prospect of his return to the oilrig making him sad. I've wrapped the sheep's skull in newspaper and stuffed it in the bottom of my suitcase, the small one with the tartan lining and shiny gold lock.

I've already finished *Treasure Island* and have hidden the map for my own buried treasure inside the book. Now I'm reading Sir Arthur Conan Doyle's *Lost World* series. I prefer Sherlock Holmes, but I've read all those, twice. Professor Challenger is sort of like a detective, too, but he's an archaeologist and explorer. When I grow up I want to travel to lost worlds like he does and discover secret grottos filled with extinct animals.

The Old Man boils eggs in a pot and forgets about them. When he takes them out of the boiling water the egg white explodes out of the cracks.

"Shite," he says. "The fecking eggs are ruined."

Mam comes out of the bedroom, wearing her pink dressing gown and slippers. She shakes her head and says, "Useless. Sure, what would you do without me? Starve, most likely."

She places three fresh eggs in the water and watches her wrist watch. The Old Man grabs her by the waist and sings, "Hey, Good Lookin', whatcha got cooking?"

She winces and pulls away from him, her face twisted. "Stop, Ronan. I'm worn out."

He sighs and sinks into the armchair by the fireplace and a minute later takes a whopper of a turf briquette, drops it on the fire and causes an explosion of sparks in the grate. Mam's two hands are on the kitchen counter and she's breathing fast and I want to ask if the baby is all right. She straightens up and takes the eggs out of the water with a spoon.

Is the brown egg she puts in the eggcup anything like the egg that's inside her, I wonder. Father Tubridy told us a sperm swims into an egg to fertilize it, but human eggs don't have hard shells like chickens do and I wonder how a rooster manages to penetrate the hard exterior of the shell with his mickey.

After I clink my spoon around the rim of the egg and open it up, the white of the egg splits and releases the yolk like glorious yellow lava. Steam rises from the cup and the smell goes up my nose. The Old Man sprinkles salt on his egg and wolfs it down, mumbling to Mam about one last trip into the village for a farewell drink. "It'll do you good to get out of the cottage," he tells her.

She makes a funny face and dabs a finger of toast into her own egg, the bright yellow yolk staining the toasted bread.

"You two should go into the village and I'll finish the packing," she says. "It's our last night in Mulrany, and the car has to be packed for the journey home."

"No. We'll all go. It's our last chance to wet the baby's head before we go back to the city," he says, happier now he's filled his belly.

"Would it kill you to stay out of the bar for one night?" Mam asks.

He thumps the table knocking over the eggcups. Mam's

eyes are full of tears, and in disbelief I watch him sweep the crockery clean off the table and onto the stone floor. The cups and saucers are in flitters and Mam has closed her eyes to his carnage.

"I'll bloody well go alone, then," he says, grabbing his coat and slamming the door on the way out. "You're useless, the fecking pair of you," he shouts back at us.

"Ah, love. He doesn't mean it," she says. "Come here to me now and we'll clean up the mess and you can read me some of your book, and then we'll all go into the village for a last drink." She goes out and tells him to hold his horses and wait for the two of us.

I am usually left in the cottage with *Treasure Island* and the wireless when they go into Mulrany for drinks at Daly's Pub, and the dark cottage, the old Ferguson transistor gets Radio Caroline and I'm able to listen to the Who and Pink Floyd as much as I want, until the revving of the engine and the crunch of gravel announces their return.

We sit at a table in the corner of the lounge and I'm given a Club Orange for a treat. Mam and the Old Man order a last round of drinks. I ask the Old Man for a bag of Quavers, but he says they'll spoil my appetite, so I sit there and watch them guzzle more Guinness and Gin and Tonics.

When I ask Mam the same question she turns to him and says, "Don't be unreasonable, Ronan." That's one of the signs she's mad at him; she uses his full name. He raps on the counter with a coin and the barman hastens our way. I'm crunching the cheesy Quavers in the corner looking at the fog rolling in from Clew Bay, Mam and the Old Man chatting with the owner, and the end of the holidays only a day or two off.

Mam finishes her gin and tonic, and the Old Man drains his whiskey in one go, tipping his cap at the barman on the way out the door. When he turns around to hold his hand out to Mam, she laughs, points at his zipper and says, "There's egg on your chin!"

And sure enough, his fly is down and his white Jockeys are visible. I say nothing at all, afraid of being given the wooden spoon for cheek. It's funny how he rolls along in the parking lot, like a headless chicken, searching his pockets for the car keys.

The Old Man loves the country life and the maze of roads he navigates in the dark brings him no end of pleasure. We take the turn for the cottage as the sun is going down and pass Loftus the postman on his Honda 50, the one that will take to the air years from now and deposit him dead in the dried-up river beneath the humpy bridge, seven children and an addled wife left behind. I hope the Old Man's not too polluted to get us home safely, but I know there's nothing to worry about because the car uncannily knows the way home without any help.

The Bunahowna River is in flood and the white-water gushes as we drive over the bridge, all of us bumping from side-to-side because of the uneven road. The sun's almost gone, but the shape of the cottage looms ahead of us in the gloom and Mam flicks the lighter and puts the tip of her cigarette to the flame.

Back in the cottage there are tiny remnants of the broken cups and eggshells on the floor of the kitchen, and like Humpty Dumpty, they can't be put back together again, and in its own way neither can our family. The Old Man is a one-man wrecking ball, and he's destroyed any hope of happiness on this our last night of the holidays.

In the morning, it's as if the events of last night never took place. The Old Man is in rare good form and we take an early morning hike down to the shore. He slaps his belly and says, "Time for a last dip, my Son of Eireann. We'll depart for home after breakfast."

"Okay," I say, and approach the waterline. I feel like a traitor, leaving Mam at the cottage folding our clothes and rustling together a last breakfast before the drive back to Dublin.

Along the empty beach seagulls struggle to make headway in the face of the strong wind and seashells tumble end over end in the wash. I pull my trunks up around my waist. The plastic buckle is a gold anchor and Mam says they look quite smart on me.

The Old Man is already up to his knees, blessing himself with the salt water and slapping a wet hand on the back of his neck. He swears this works to ease the cold, but when I try the same thing a wave washes over my belly and I have goose bumps covering my entire body. In one clumsy motion, I crab dive into the sharp Atlantic, the water sliding over me, and the Old Man laughing at my awkwardness.

I am an explorer on the verge of a great discovery. I pull the blue plastic goggles over my eyes and look through the glass at the sandy bottom for unidentified sea creatures. I invent these games where I imagine the pair of us as a team, intrepid adventurers. The Old Man does not indulge me. Instead he travels parallel to the shoreline, one arm triangled over the waves, then the other, pulling himself along in the water.

Maybe I did something to hurt him when I was a small boy, or maybe he knows I've been stealing change from his pants in the mornings. It hurts not to have a dad who does dad things with me. How hard can it be to talk to your only son, to share your feelings about life and not just bottle them in until they boil over in anger like the other night in the kitchen?

A dead seahorse floats in the water and I pluck it out and hold it against the sky. Curved like an "S" from a storybook, the seahorse is a beautiful thing. I take my goggles off and fill them with water. Then I place the seahorse in one eye socket. Sand washes off its body and its purple-ribbed corpse shines in the sunlit water. I wade back to shore; afraid I'll crush it.

Back at the cottage Mam reads the newspaper and smokes another cigarette, the breakfast made, suitcases packed and ready at the door. The baby is in its house, waiting to be born. When I show Mam the tiny creature in my goggles she says she's never seen one so lovely.

"It's wonderful. Thank you for sharing it with me." She yawns, sleepy from last night at the pub.

After breakfast, I bury the seahorse in the rocky area by the fence. I stand over the mound of stones and say a prayer for the maritime traveler and toast its return to nothingness. When I get back to the cottage the Old Man is crunching on dried toast with corned beef slices from the grocery and dripping butter on Mam's *Sunday Independent*.

"Sit down and eat something more. It's a long drive back," Mam says. "Won't you be delighted to get back to the city and your pals and DeValera?"

"Yes, Mam. I can't wait to see Tommy again," I reply, eating a slice of toast and marmalade.

"Run off now and make sure you're leaving nothing behind," Mam says.

When I'm sure I have all my stuff and there's nothing left in the little bedroom at the back of the cottage, I say, "Give me one tick," and run back to the seahorse's grave to say goodbye to the summer.

The dead creature makes me sad. What if I drowned in the ocean? Where would I be now? Maybe in the grounds of Athleague Cemetery on the Ballygar Road with a headstone over me like my grandparents and the Old Man's young sisters who died at 5 and 14. The inscription might say something like, *Beloved Son of Ronan and Helen Brogan: an explorer to the end.*

I don't want to be dead, though. They say you go to Heaven, or Purgatory if you've done some wicked things and need some time to amend for your sins before they allow you inside the pearly gates.

All the stars in the sky are dead souls, wandering the universe waiting for their turn to get into Heaven, and each time one shoots across the sky it's on its way home. This idea comforts me when I think about death and dying. It's nice to know there's somewhere your friends can look to see if you're out there in space, floating, waiting, and hanging on until the moment of salvation arrives.

We'll be on the road in a jiffy according to Mam. She's busy sorting the last of the Old Man's socks into pairs and folding them into the suitcase. I can't wait to get back to the avenue and hear all about how Tommy got on with minding DeValera whilst we were away. I've been missing the dog something awful.

The roof rack helter-skelters on top of the Austin Wolseley as we ready for the drive back to Dublin. "Hurrah for shite," The Old Man says, as he knots the rope holding the suitcases down. I slip away to the back of the cottage one last time and look out on the wide world of Clew Bay and the tiny islands dotting the ocean.

The tangle of gorse bushes behind the cottage where I found the skull is covered by early morning mist, and down the bottom of the hill is the spot where I buried the coins. The faint green moss shines on the rocky wall and I wish we weren't going home today. The Old Man wanders over to the gorse bushes and I can hear the stream of his pee as he relieves himself in the shadows. We'll be home in time for tea unless he takes too many detours to wet his whistle.

Mam is inside cleaning the kitchen one last time. The baby has been kicking her tummy hard for two days now and she's taken to calling it "her little angel."

The Old Man pops the boot of the car open to load the bedclothes Mam has washed and folded. She has scrubbed the kitchen and put out the fire in the stove. Mam wants to linger, and runs a hand along the counter by the fridge, as if remembering where everything is for some reason.

The dog across the road barks at the Old Man as he walks up the driveway to give a check for our rent to the owners of the cottage. When he comes back down the driveway his shoes crunch on the gravel and the dog leaps in the air at his side. The smell of whiskey is on his breath, and he must have had a quick one with Mr. Coughlan, the owner.

"I gave them the same dates for next year," he says to Mam. "Sure, there's nowhere like it in the world. God's grandeur indeed."

Mam doesn't respond, and he must be getting the silent treatment for coming back with booze on his breath. I finger the pimple on my chin and take a last look out at Clew Bay in front of us, the Atlantic Ocean stretching all the way to America. The Old Man pretends to punch me and puts his fist to my jaw. I smile at him and he winks. We drive off with the dust from the road kicking up behind the car, and as we pass Loftus the postman's house with his seven children and frantic wife, the Old Man honks the horn three times in salute.

We stop in Athleague Cemetery to visit the dead relatives, and one thing leads to another, and a detour to Baltrasna to see some old family members who live in a doomed mansion with ivy creeper all over the walls, even on the inside. A great-aunt and uncle I've never seen before give me whiskery kisses on the cheek and the Old Man chuckles as they comment on how I'm "a chip off the old block."

My great uncle's name is Matt and he has shallow breathing and a long, loud wheeze. Great-Aunt Mary explains he's recently gotten over heart surgery. She is a little bird bouncing around the kitchen pulling cups and saucers from cupboards and setting a blackened kettle to boil on the range. I ask her where the toilet is and disappear up the stairs in the entryway.

In a corner of an upstairs room I find an old flying helmet and a bunch of rusted golf clubs. I take the helmet from the floor and try it on. The leather smells musty and is cracked in places, but the goggles still have glass in the lenses, and I secure the strap under my chin the way it's meant to be cinched. I stuff the helmet down my pants and hope it doesn't get seen.

We drive off well after eight o'clock as the crows fly home for the evening. Soon, Mam is snoring next to the Old Man, and I'm squinting at the small print in my new book as the miles are gobbled up under the wheels of the Austin Wolseley.

Finally, we're shuttling through the outskirts of the city, the Rowntree Mackintosh factory has a few windows lit up in the night, and I wonder if the conveyor belts that carry the fruit pastilles are silent now everyone's gone home for the day? Maybe there are rats running here and there, feral eyes in the darkness, nibbling on crystals of sugar missed by the cleaning crew.

The Old Man's eyebrows are like giant caterpillars. I see them in the rear-view mirror and his brow is knitted in concentration as he steers us through the empty streets of Dublin. Mam dreams of things I'll never know anything about: personal things, like her old boyfriend, the Bird. I breathe on the window and draw two stick figures with my finger—a woman and a bird, kissing.

As we drive over Crossguns Bridge Mam wakes up and says, "I might have a bit of a fever."

The Old Man snorts and says she must be bewildered. The bridge is in darkness and maybe there are foxes and badgers hiding in the shadows, waiting for their prey.

Our street is empty and it's late. The smell of the coast is no longer in the air, and there's something a little sad about our red-bricked house in front of us. The windows are heavy with sleep, and after I help unload the car I retreat to my bedroom and hide the stolen helmet at the back of the wardrobe, under the moth-eaten fur coat that belongs to Auntie Martha.

In the kitchen, Mam rattles the cups and saucers to knock the dust of two weeks off. "A cup of tea is just what the doctor ordered," she says. The Old Man twists the foil top off the whiskey bottle and pours a glassful, his hand shaking.

"Would you like a ham sandwich?" Mam asks.

"Arrah, not at all. Couldn't you put on a bit of a fry?"

Mam bangs the kettle on the cooker and slams the cutlery drawer shut. "Do you think I'm a fecking skivvy? I spent the entire holiday cooking and cleaning just like the rest of the year. Where's my holiday, I want to know?"

Mam doesn't often use bad language, but when she does it usually means a huge fight is coming.

I make a beeline for my bedroom and decide to organize the books on my bookshelf into alphabetic order. Adams, Richard. *Watership Down*. Mam gave me that one for my birthday last year, and I still haven't opened it up. I decide right then that I'm going to read that book before I go back to school, and that I'll be able to write a great book report on it for my English class for next year's competition.

Mam and the Old Man are yelling downstairs about fairness, and the cupboards are getting slammed as usual. With a pillow held over my head I can muffle out most of the noise, and there's a chance I'll end up smothering myself and won't have to tolerate their bickering any more.

I go down for my tea and I can't believe the Old Man is back to his usual nonsense. I was praying our time looking at the stars and walking the strand at Mulrany was the change I've dreamt of, but I must be stupid to think he'd change so easily. He's set in his ways, and like Mam says, "A leopard can't change its spots."

"Well, well, well," The Old Man says, as the RTE Newsflash

announces President DeValera's death. "The Chief is dead! God forgive me, but I hope the coals of hell scorch his fecking arse."

Mam shakes her head and makes the Sign of the Cross. "We'll say a prayer for him, no matter his politics," she says. The Old Man begrudgingly blesses himself and we say a Decade of the Rosary for the repose of his soul.

The radio and TV play nothing but programs about how DeValera brought Ireland into the 20th Century and when an announcer suggests he was one of Ireland's greatest sons, the Old Man shouts at the screen, "He wasn't fecking Irish at all. He was a bloody Yank!"

"Simmer down, Ronan," Mam says, switching the TV off and motioning for me to go to bed.

A couple of days later, Mam and I watch the funeral on RTE, the cortege driving past the GPO and finally the interment in Glasnevin Cemetery. The Old Man has taken refuge in the pub, determined to play no part in witnessing the death of a hero.

Chapter 12

Our walks start in September; awkward things around nearby neighborhoods, far enough away from either of our houses. Mrs. Prendergast is a lady with a sharp tongue and a quick hand, and Cathy says she often gets a palm across the face for her trouble—that's why we sneak about—walking in the shadows of the tall trees by the cottages in Irishtown, where we'll never be spotted.

Cathy's hand is like Velcro in mine, and she's delighted to be with me, away from her family. We have a connection, a way of "getting" each other that surprises us both. At the top of the avenue a fuchsia bush hangs over the wall, red flowers cascading everywhere. Cathy holds my hand and says, "I need to go in now. Mammy will be looking for me."

She leans in and kisses my cheek. I redden, shocked, and turn towards her and put my lips to hers. She squeezes my hand and says, "See you later."

I float up the avenue all the way to our front door, my head spinning with thoughts of her soft lips. I cannot say a word to my parents because I can already hear the Old Man's mockery, "Georgie Porgie pudding and pie, kissed the girls and made them cry…"

Cathy is my secret, my secret from his cruel teasing. Still, in the cold night air, shoveling coal into the scuttle, my thoughts are of her tongue in my mouth, soft kisses, our eyes open and watching for familiar faces in unfamiliar places. So, in the backyard, I watch the neighbor's cat flop down on the garage roof, a mouse in its paws, and a string of entrails purple in moonlight. The cat is the Old Man, and the mouse is me, and I hate the way he makes me feel stupid and childish.

Lying on my bed later, I laugh. My heart does weird flips as I recall the taste of her lips. The way the freckles dot her cheeks, the long, translucent eyelashes, and her hair pulled back behind the ears; I know I like her way too much already.

When I go downstairs, Mam must see the look on my face because she says, "You look like the cat that ate the cream." The knitting needle is between her teeth, and the yarn unravels, row by mistaken row, on the carpet. "Go on now, and fetch in some more fuel before the rain starts again."

I take the coal scuttle to the backyard, where threaded webs hang down from the timbers of the coal shed, their occupants tight in the corners, bright-eyed spiders with nasty tongues.

The blade of the shovel chips shards from the coal and when the scuttle fills it's as if it were loaded with cement.

"It'll make you stronger," the Old Man says.

When I complain of the knot in my shoulder he sneers at me and asks, "Are you a man or a mouse?"

No point responding, so I accept his barb and his thick fingers poke bruises in my ribs to make me less of a complainer. I wish I could stand up to him. I hate how he pushes me around and makes fun of me because I'm not as tough as him. It doesn't matter, because Cathy is great and I like her a lot, and like kissing her, and I think she's going to be my first real girlfriend. I can't ever tell Mam or the Old Man why I am so happy, because I am her little soldier, and if she knew what I was up to she'd skin me alive.

The Old Man is leaving to go back to the oilrig soon and school is back in session and I've got my Intermediate Certificate exams this coming June. I'm going to have to study extra-hard because I'll be expected to help Mam out more with the new baby, and although the Old Mam's been promising to help Mam out around the house as she gets things ready for the baby, the reality is that he disappears early in the day and reappears almost by magic when Mam is putting meals on the table.

I take DeValera out to the garden so she can do her business, and when I go back inside, the Old Man says he's going to make breakfast because Mam isn't feeling well. He rattles about the kitchen, uncertain of where any of the utensils are located. Even the idea of making breakfast is momentous for him. He is not able to cook, and the smell of burning meat fills the kitchen and thick smoke pours along the narrow passage leading to the front hall. When he brings Mam the breakfast on a plate she sends him away with his burnt offerings and turns her face into the pillow.

I kiss her goodbye and head off to school, where classes go by slowly; Latin, Biology, Irish History, and English before lunch. After lunch, it's Maths and Civics and French with Monsieur Deane. He wears his dust cover like Batman's cape, but he's so wishy-washy nobody can see him as the super-hero type. He's a total snob and addresses the students as "Peasants." Everyone loves how he treats us like fools, always looking down his snooty nose at us and saying, "Assiyez-vous, maggots."

I cycle home in the rain, my face stung by the force of

the wind and the water gets inside my rain gear because the lining has lost its waterproof coating. I'll have to have a hot bath the minute I get home, or Mam will tell me I'll end up in the hospital with pneumonia.

Mam is at the kitchen table in a blouse the color of a ruined meadow. She is silent and dabs at her wet cheeks. When I ask her what's wrong, she says she's going to miss the Old Man. I'm confused with how she says she loves him one minute, and the next she can't abide even the mention of his name. I wish I knew more about what happened to make us leave our old house and come to the city. As far as I can tell Mam is in love with the "idea" of the Old Man, and not the person himself.

She says the Old Man was never happier than when he was behind the bar pulling pints and telling stories for his pals. I don't remember much of those days at all. I do remember the bantam hens in the backyard and their pecking and clucking all the time, and I remember the time I pulled a bag of quicklime down on my head. The lime turned the skin behind my ears raw red, and Mam and Aunt Martha spent long nights boiling water and placing poultices on the sores. It took four months for the lime-damaged skin to heal and it cost a fortune in prescriptions from the local pharmacy.

She notices the state of my clothes and tells me to get into the bath before I catch my death. "I'm going to take a lie down," she says, getting up and shuffling across the kitchen towards the hall.

I want to comfort her, so I make her a mug of tea. When I bring her the mug she's lying on the bedcovers and I have to help her sit up straight because of the bump. I can tell she hurts because her face changes when she shifts position. Mam sips at the hot tea and says, "Will you bring me the lighter from my purse? I'm gasping for a fag."

I find the purse in her handbag, underneath a paperback Ngaio Marsh mystery with a strange redheaded woman on the cover. Mam's eyes are half-closed, so I take the mug of tea from her hands and put it beside the lighter.

Mam's eyes are puffy from dragging the extra weight of the baby around the house while she tidies things. I give her a hug and when I go downstairs I take the Cadbury's tin from the cupboard and slice off a bit of orange sponge cake. She is the best baker in the world, and when it's my birthday I get a real birthday cake with fancy decoration all around it. Tommy's ma buys shop-made cakes from Eaton's and the TeaTime Express in town, and those cakes aren't half as good as Mam's.

I run a bath and the toilet fills with steam, the mirror clouded and dripping with condensation. I fill the tub with Radox and when I slide into the water I disappear into the bubbles. Until the water cools down I lie there with my eyes closed wondering about the Old Man and his anger, and how he keeps it on the boil like a pot on the stove, ready to spill over at any time. I hope I don't act like he does when I grow up. I clamber out of the tub and drip suds on the linoleum floor.

I run another bath for Mam, because I know it's good for her to be able to relax and not think of stressful things. I wake her and eventually she disappears into the bathroom, cigarette in hand.

The bathroom door is open as usual, and when I catch sight of her in the steamy light after her bath, her belly sticks out a mile and has hundreds of wrinkles on it, like the hide of the old elephant in the Dublin Zoo. The rest of her body is misshapen and thin. When she sees me looking she grabs the towel and covers herself, her eyes dim and a faraway look on her face. She shuts the door and I go and eat my cake in the quiet of my bedroom.

I flick through the box of albums beside my record player. I found Steely Dan's LP, *Pretzel Logic* in the bargain bin at Golden Discs last week and bought it for fifty pence. The

148

cover is weird, because the word pretzel is spelled, "pretzle." The music is odd and I'm not sure I like it at all the first time I play it, but I'm sick of listening to Jackson Browne, so I put the record on the turntable and place the needle in the groove.

As I listen to "*Rikki Don't Lose That Number*," the hall door bangs and the Old Man roars up the stairs for me to turn down the "Jungle Music." Once the record is back in its sleeve I go down to see him.

"Have you no consideration for your poor mother?" he says. "She needs plenty of rest for the baby and you're playing your hurdy-gurdy as if everything is hunky-dory."

I blush, say sorry, and tell him Mam's resting after her bath and he'll wake her if he's not quiet.

"Get out of my sight before I tan your hide," he says, disappearing into the sitting room to watch Don Cockburn read the evening news on RTE. In my room, I look through a book of Byzantine paintings that belonged to Mam when she was in school. There are strange buildings with crescents and gold domes and if I could magic myself out of this world and back in time, I would.

All of September, Mam works like a madwoman to knit all sorts of booties and blankets for the new arrival. I'm supposed to go to the church to say my confession, since I've made my Confirmation and am now a bona fide Catholic.

On the balcony above the church door the choir practices with Ms. Fox. As I bend over the altar rail to say my penance, rather than close my eyes the way I'm meant to, I sneak a look at Cathy, who's on the end of the row, her hair pulled back with the ladybird barrette I always tease her about. She doesn't like it when I make fun of her, and I know she got the barrette from her dead sister's jewelry box. She sees me looking at her and tries to keep a straight face, but when I stick out my tongue she laughs and Ms. Fox, the choir teacher rattles her baton against the wooden lectern. The Old Man says Ms. Fox is well named because she resembles one, with her red hair and the way her nose twitches when she looks at you.

"An examination of my conscience," the priest says. I sit in the wooden pew while he waits for me to grade my sins into some order or other.

"Bless me Father for I have sinned. It's been six weeks since my last confession."

"Go on, my son," the voice behind the grille says.

My knees hurt from the hard leather pad, hands joined, eyes closed. I knew I was going to lie, even before I got into the confession box.

"I stole money from my Mam's purse. And I took the Lord's name in vain," I say in a croaky voice.

"Is that all, my son?" He coughs, and I catch a glimpse of his gold Crucifix glinting in the light. "Are you sure?"

"Yes, Father."

"Say your Act of Contrition, and for your penance, three Hail Marys and a Hail Holy Queen." He mutters the *Te Absolvo* as I singsong the Act of Contrition. "O, My God, I am heartily sorry..."

I kissed Cathy Prendergast under the fuchsia bush at the top of our road. I played with my yoke and it leaked on the sheets.

I hope Cathy doesn't say anything to the priest when she makes her confession. What if she tells him about our kiss? He'll batter me stupid next time I see him.

After choir practice, Cathy says she'll meet me later if I can get out of the house, so I run home and tell Mam that I'll be going over to Tommy's house to study.

I get on my bike with my headphones on, threating to blow my eardrums to smithereens. " When you see me coming you had better run run run from Dearg Doom," Horslips blare.

Within five minutes of leaving the house the sky goes from clear blue to stony gray. I fly by the School of Driving, past the pizza joint that does no business, and past a Chinese Restaurant. The painted dragon eyes me out of the heavy rain, the spray flumes from the back wheel, like an uncoiled tail of dirty water.

"How's it going?" I say, skidding to a semi-circular halt in front of her.

"You scared me!" she says, her fingers playing with the end of her school scarf, picking at the frayed bits of wool. She stares down at her shoes while I talk—Cathy in her gabardine overcoat and lustrous black hair.

"Sorry. Want to go to the park?" I ask.

"That'd be nice." She stands up and swings the scarf across her shoulder.

There are butterflies in my stomach.

She walks off, heading to the park. We make our way along the Dodder, the water gushing past. She doesn't have much to say. Words stick my throat and I'm afraid to speak, certain to say the wrong thing. At the arsenal, we walk up to the parapets like in a real castle and look over the edge at the drop.

"Do you want to kiss me again?" she asks. "It was nice last time, but we had to go home too soon." She pulls me by the hand towards the wall. I don't know what to say, so I lean towards her and she tilts her head. I close my eyes and pretend it's her mother I'm kissing instead, her sexy perfume and her blouse wide open. I try to stop these ideas because it feels like I'm betraying Cathy.

Our lips touch and I can taste her strawberry lip-gloss, sweet and wet. I try to get my tongue past but she puts two hands on my shoulders and pushes me away. "I've got to get home for tea before my parents get into it again," she says.

We part at the top of our road, not wanting to be seen together. If my old man were to see me with a girl he'd never let me hear the end of it.

"Can we do this again?" I ask, secretly wanting to just see

her mother.

Cathy smiles. The scarf covers her mouth, but I know she's smiling by the way the corners of her eyes crinkle with these tiny lines. "Why not?" She scuffs the toe of her shoe on the ground and watches me with her blue eyes.

When Mam goes up to bed I take the telephone into the dining room and dial Cathy's number. She answers and we spend the next hour-and-a-half whispering into the phone to each other. I tell her all about Mam's baby and how I hope it comes soon, and she cries as she tells me all the terrible things her father does to her mother when he's angry. She must fall asleep while we're still on the phone, because she doesn't say anything for a long time, and when I say her name there's silence. I hang up, replace the phone on the hall table and tiptoe up to my bedroom.

Dublin, wet and dreary, winter twelve months of the year even though it's autumn, the sunless void, and the Old Man is rotten with drink in the company of our token relatives, John Power and Arthur Guinness, there for a Sunday visit. He leaves to go back to the oilrig in the morning.

We're sitting at the breakfast table when DeValera comes into the kitchen with the Old Man's best fishing rod, the bamboo one that belonged to my grandfather, in her mouth. The Old Man sees the splintered mess on the floor of the pantry and loses his rag. He chases the dog with the remains of the rod and whales into the beast with the handle. Poor DeValera whimpers in the corner by the back door.

"Leave the poor creature alone," Mam says, washing the dishes in the sink.

"That dog has to go. I'll put a stop to her gallop and no mistake," he says, pushing the dog out the back door. DeValera cowers inside the doghouse, paws over her eyes. I'm perched on the kitchen stool watching from the window as the Old

Man grabs the coal shovel and brings it down on her head.

I scream, and Mam takes me in her arms and shushes me. The crunch is terrible, and I look away as he hits her again and again. Mam tries to pull me away from the window. The dog's barking stops, and the Old Man drags her out of her house by the collar. Her body is limp and her head all bloodied.

Mam says, "Look away, for the love of God."

The Old Man has murdered DeValera, and I'm sick to my stomach.

"He's a desperate man, your father. I don't know what gets into him," she says.

I want to bring the shovel down on *his* skull and see what he thinks of being murdered by someone.

When he reappears from the backyard, I'm screaming at him. "I hate you! I hope you die. You're an awful person."

He wipes the sweat from his forehead with his coat sleeve, and says, "Get out of my sight. That dog was always queer in the head."

I go upstairs to my room and curl up on the bed until suppertime.

There's a fresh mound of dirt beside the garden shed where the Old Man has buried DeValera without even a cross.

Mam brings him his nightcap as usual, her duty to serve. His poison is a boilermaker of Guinness and Powers, supped with relish.

I seethe in the corner, hoping he'll die of a heart attack.

She purses her lips at the noises he makes downing his drink.

But I stay silent. I fear he will explode and club my ears to a pulp if I bring up the subject. But suddenly I don't care. I hate him. He murdered DeValera.

I take the hammer from the pantry and smash the wireless set to smithereens. My blows send it toppling to the floor. Hilversum, Budapest, Eireann, Brussels, and Munich, all the stations of the airwaves shatter into pieces of brown glass.

Over and over, I rain down hammer blows on the radio, sing-songing, "I hate you, you bastard."

"Ah, you omadhaun," he yells, trying to grab the hammer from my hands. He cuffs me with his patched elbow and sends me spinning to the ground. "The fecking wireless is banjaxed. Have you no sense at all?"

I hold the hammer up and yell, "If you hit me one more time I'll smash your head in. You're nothing but a bully and a murderer and the poor dog didn't deserve to die like that."

His hands fall to his sides and he shunts the remains of the wireless with his foot.

"Have you any idea of the price of these bloody wireless sets?" he asks.

"It's only money, love," Mam says, defending me for once.

"Money! Do you think it grows on bloody trees?" he shouts. "And me on the oilrigs working like a dog to provide for the pair of ye?"

"I don't care. You killed DeValera and I hope you die, too," I say. I drop the hammer to the ground and disappear to my bedroom, leaving the Old Man in the midst of a sea of broken glass and plastic.

In the morning, Mam knocks on my door and says the Old Man is ready to leave for the oilrig and won't I say good-bye to him, anyway.

I lean against the door and say, "I'm not talking to him. For all I care I hope he drowns in the North Sea." Her footsteps recede and I go to the window where I see him load his duffel bag in the back of a taxicab. He looks up at the window and I pull back so he can't see me. Only when the taxicab draws away from the curb do I return to the window and catch him looking out the back window.

"Fuck you," I say to myself.

I throw myself down on my bed and cry my eyes out for poor DeValera. How the Old Man was able to kill the dog without any remorse terrifies me.

The eye of the needle glints sliver in the pale light from the corner lamp as Mam licks the thread and attempts to pass it through the narrow opening. Its late afternoon, the fire's blazing, and outside it's pelting down. I'm halfway through *David Copperfield*, the small print making my eyes hurt. Mam says Charles Dickens was a genius. The coal spits against the fireguard and Mam says to watch out for sparks. My elbow hurts from where I've been leaning on it and my foot has pins and needles.

I'm finishing the chapter when Mam gets up and goes to the kitchen to boil the kettle for tea.

"Patrick!" She yells from the kitchen.

When I get there she's pale and clutches her handbag in both hands. "We've been robbed! My children's allowance book is gone, and the money I got from the post office today."

The kitchen door is shut, but someone's got in through the broken window the Old Man hasn't gotten around to fixing.

"I swear it was those tinkers who came about the other week on their cart. They've spent it already on beer I don't wonder."

"Phone the guards," I tell her. "Maybe they can get fingerprints off the window, or your handbag."

She looks at me as if I've said something hilarious. "Fingerprints? There's no use taking fingerprints. It's not one of your detective stories. Didn't I ask you to shut that window?" She slams the press door shut and rattles the glass jar of tealeaves before taking a loaf of bread from the breadbox. After a few moments she says, "Maybe you're right. I'll phone the station in Rathmines."

Up the hall she goes and the burr of the phone dial repeats until she says, "Hello, I'd like to report a theft."

Two uniformed men are at the door within the hour and

they follow Mam into the kitchen. After she shows them the window they look closely at the glass, shake their heads and examine the open space between the window and the ledge.

One of them scratches his nose and says, "It must have been a child to get in that narrow distance."

The other one licks the stub of a pencil and writes in a small notebook. He looks up and says, "It's a familiar problem with those bloody tinkers, Missus. We've had three break-ins around here lately."

Mam folds the open *Evening Press* and attempts to kill a bluebottle crawling up the wall.

"At a minimum, I'd fix that window; it's an open invitation for burglars. And keep the allowance book and money somewhere safer than a handbag," the guard says.

Mam crinkles her eyes and replies, "Sure, if you can't be safe in your own home..."

The two guards tip their caps and leave without any further words.

"I'm sure that bloody pair think this is hilarious," Mam says, when the door shuts behind them. "Well, it'll be baked beans on toast for tea until next children's allowance day." She sets to the Batchelor's baked beans, her vengeance taken out on the can-opener. "Your father will lose his reason when he hears about this," she says, tipping the beans into a Pyrex dish and turning on the oven.

"Maybe we shouldn't tell him, so it doesn't upset him?" I suggest to Mam.

"Let me deal with this," she replies. "I don't want to be worrying him all the way in the wilds of the North Sea." I say nothing at all; more interested in returning to Dickens' London town than in wondering how we've been duped by the tinkers.

We're declining verbs when Kevin Corcoran, Dean of

Third Year, sticks his walrus-mustached face around the door.

"Sorry Father Colley, could I have Mr. Brogan," he asks.

The priest nods, the large mole on his face moving in agreement. When I go outside Mam is waiting for me in her overcoat, the scarf tied tight under her chin. She's pale, and looks like she's been crying.

"Your Da's been in an accident."

"Is it bad? Is he dead?"

"No. He's being airlifted to the mainland. I'm getting the ferry tonight and I'll be in Aberdeen tomorrow."

Immediately I regret ever wishing him dead and I know what I said when he killed DeValera and I wish I could take it back. If he dies it will be all my fault. How will I survive knowing I murdered my father? I offer a silent Hail Mary that he recovers and comes home to us in once piece.

The Dean puts a hand on my shoulder and motions me back to class to pick up my stuff. As I grab my schoolbag from the desk the lads are whispering, but I walk out and put my hand in Mam's. The taxi driver puts my bicycle in the boot of the car and we drive home in silence. Mam says Auntie Martha will come to take care of me while she's in Scotland making sure the Old Man is all right. She whispers that Uncle Harry and Aunt Martha are not getting along and it'll be good for her to get away from him for a while. I'm too afraid to whinge, or ask what she means about "not getting along." She hugs me to her chest and says the Old Man will soon be home safe and sound.

The details are lost on me, but Mam says a loose traveling block plummeted from the derrick and crushed his hip into pulp. He will have nine surgeries and endure a long, steel implant with six stainless steel screws inserted in his thigh. Auntie Martha is in transit and as soon as she arrives Mam will be off in a taxi to the ferry.

There's no avoiding mortality now. The Old Man is going to die and it's all my fault for wishing it on him. Why couldn't

I have forgiven him for the moment of madness when he clobbered DeValera with the shovel? Part of me knows he's getting what he deserves, because there's no way you're meant to hurt a poor, defenseless dog.

Mam and I wait in the warmth of the kitchen for Aunt Martha. Neither of us has much to say. The Westclox above the Aga ticks out the minutes. I stare at the ceiling where the waxy wallpaper has yellowed from years of cooking grease and cigarette smoke.

If he dies, the Old Man's ghost will surely inhabit the layers of grease thick on the walls. Mam holds herself with both arms wrapped about her shoulders, the headscarf tied tight under her chin. Our shared fear inhabits the silence like a dismal fog off the Irish Sea. I cross the kitchen and hug her, and tell her I am sorry for causing his accident.

"Ah, love. It wasn't anything you did that caused it at all," she says.

The honk of the taxi startles us and I open the door for Auntie Martha. I haven't seen her since Granny's funeral and she looks thinner, older, and a little yellow in the face.

"My old segosha," she says, and kisses me with her whiskery lips. "God love you all." "Give your old aunt a proper kiss," she says, and offers me her rouged cheek again. Auntie Martha has stubble like the Old Man's, and it hurts my lips when I kiss her. She also smells like the inside of the old suitcase on top of the wardrobe in my bedroom.

"Your auntie will be staying on while your Da is in hospital," Mam says. "She'll give me a hand until the baby arrives. Uncle Harry can manage the shop with the girls who work there. Your dinner is in the oven," she says. "I'll phone from Aberdeen to let you know how he is."

"My, my," Martha croons, as she puts an arm around my waist, "You're growing into a fine lad, altogether."

Mam waves at us from the taxi window as it drives off in a spume of mist.

I flee upstairs to my bedroom and lie on the floor with *David Copperfield*. Later, when I go to pee in the bathroom there are brown stockings hanging from the shower curtain. I smell the toe of one of them and it has the same pong as Auntie Martha's old suitcase.

"Aren't you a grand big lad, now," she says, coming into the bathroom as I'm washing my hands. She rubs my shoulders from behind. "You love your old Aunt Martha, don't you?"

Her body presses into mine and I don't like how it makes me feel. "I have to run and do my homework," I say, pulling away from her and escaping back up the small flight of stairs to my bedroom. As I do my homework on the bed I can hear the low moans of her cello coming from the spare room beside the toilet. It sounds so sad and lonely, as I imagine Auntie Martha must feel inside.

During the night, the house creaks and groans like a geriatric, the floorboards settle and the North wind tears strips off the country from top to bottom. I toss from side-to-side in the bed, Auntie Martha's snores mixing with the howls of wind, and I fall asleep and dream of DeValera's skeleton chasing the Old Man around the garden.

Chapter 13

The Old Man returns to Dublin a week later and because Mam can't drive, our neighbor with the stiff leg, John Carson, transports us through the freezing night fog to the hospital, the old lampposts looming up out of the ground as I imagine trees do in mangrove swamps. The lights themselves radiate colored circles of energy and glow eerie in the fog. While we visit the hospital Mr. Carson stays sitting on the bonnet of his car smoking his Woodbine cigarettes.

I burst into tears when I see the Old Man, pulleys in a cage-like bed—limbs suspended—his face blue-black, the right leg held in mid-air by steel cords, the right arm encased in plaster, his bruised eyes; the yellowed skin and heavy scabbing from the accident make him appear almost comatose. I move close to the bed and touch the plaster cast on his arm and tell how I went to Mass and prayed for him, and how I'm sorry for wishing him harm. I still cannot forgive him for what he did to DeValera, but I'm relieved he hasn't died because of me.

The Old Man says it was a mistake, nothing more, the slip, and then the massive weight of the traveling block crushing his femur into pieces. "I was thinking of your Mam's Yorkshire puddings and not minding my business," he says. Lucky for him the supply helicopter was on the platform at the time and was able to airlift him to the mainland without delay.

Mam cries from the Birth of the Virgin Mary to the Canonization of Blessed Oliver Plunkett, her voice diminished to a low quaver, her grip on things less sure by the day.

The rehab takes place at The National Rehab Clinic in Dun Laoghaire, not the same place she sent him a few years back to dry his liver out for the Christmas. We visit and I wave from the car window to the figure in the top floor window. I can't tell if he nods, or whether the shape in the window is the Old Man. Mr. Carson drives us in the old Wolseley, the one with the black trim on the body.

The Old Man comes home on a chilly October afternoon. The ambulance deposits him at the house, and the two uniformed men wheel him into the dining room on a gurney. We have moved his bedroom downstairs and Mam has bought an orthopedic bed. They transfer him from wheelchair to bed, the massive steel implant that holds his femur together shines in the late-autumn sun that filters through the window.

His left pajama leg is slit to the thigh and beneath is the exposed flesh where the steel implant weighs him down. Three round holes the shape of a ten-penny pieces are driven into his leg. He winks at me when he sees my eyes fixed on his wounds.

In the weeks since he's been home he limps about the garden with his six-iron, and nods at the neighbors. It is as if he is a wild animal trapped in a cage, his gait unsteady, as he trudges about the ten square feet of grass. The hospital walker rusts in the back garden and over time turns into a makeshift frame for Mam's sweet peas.

Mam goes to the Church, her hair in a net, the cigarette red-tipped in her teeth. She is convinced if the Old Man prays more and goes on retreat he will return to his full glory. When she comes home she has the parish priest with her, and the look on his face is all business.

The Old Man's face crumples into wet tissue when he sees the priest. Father McDaid is a small dour man, with spaghetti-thin legs and a shiny domed head, pitted and scarred like the moon's surface. Mam opens the gate, touches the Old Man's shoulder, and steers him towards the door.

"How are you, Son?" the priest asks me.

"Grand, Father. I'm off to play soccer with my pals," I tell him, and run for the lane across the street.

"Well, good luck then," he says, and follows my parents into the house.

When the door closes, I sneak back across the road and slip inside. They're all in the kitchen and the door is closed, but I can hear the Old Man's complaints about his knees and how they're ruined from the accident. I put my ear to the door because I can't hear the priest's voice, but when I do, he says, "You must pray daily, Ronan. Say an Our Father, and the Boss Man will look after your soul."

"My soul, Father?" He grunts. "It's my gammy leg I'm worried about."

Mam rattles the kettle on the hob, and the sound of the match as it ignites the gas to flame is loud. I try to imagine the red heat on my arm and the flames as they lick my skin. I don't feel sick, but when I see fire a strange sensation comes over me.

"Ronan, these are dark days, sent by God to test your faith. You must find solace in the darkness, light in the worst moments of despair. Isn't your good wife here in desperate need of you now that the baby's almost due?"

Father McDaid is a great man for the despair. His black shirt has snowdrifts of dandruff on it and he scratches at his bald head all the time. He visited the house once a week while the Old Man was on the rig, and left his dandruff like confetti on the kitchen table for Mam to sweep up and put in the bin.

"Father," she says, "Do you think we might have Ronan go to Lough Derg for a retreat when he's a bit more mobile?"

"Oh, a turn around the rocks of the island would be quite the thing, but that'll be when his injuries have mended," the priest says. "I'm not sure he's up to it yet."

"I'm a long way from mended," he says. "I'll be back on my feet soon enough, and well able to chase the missus around the garden!"

"God forgive you," Mam says, and the whistle of the kettle drowns out whatever else is said.

The priest says, "I've to get home for my own tea, now."

Right then the door opens and the priest sees me on my knees.

"The plot thickens," he says with a wink.

He disappears out the door and off home for his tea.

In the night, I wait for the Old Man to die, for the last breath to flee his body and for DeValera's revenge to be exacted. The darkness brings an opportunity to relieve myself of the burden of anger. Each night the light from the streetlamp outside seeps through the scrim of curtains and my careful monitoring of his existence continues into the small hours until I cannot help but fall asleep.

In the coal-black night, I listen for the snores, the stutter of the in-breath: a pause, then the exhalation. Too often my nights are consumed by the longing. My intuition tells me the out breath is going to stop and not be followed by an intake. Then he will be dead and I'll be free of the pathological guilt of wanting his death, so my sleep can go untroubled. I yearn for him to die, a patient vigil that never ends.

I wonder what the priest would say in the confession box if I told him the awful thoughts I have about the Old Man's death? He'd give me enough Decades of the Rosary as penance to keep me busy for years.

Auntie Martha returns to help Mam get ready for the new baby. Mam and the Old Man are away for the day for Mam's maternity hospital check-up. The Old Man felt well enough to go with her. and said he was sick of moping about the house. It's another warm October day and already Aunt Martha is asleep in the sitting room.

I'm in the back garden with Tommy ogling the Dempsey's trees, which sport some large shiny fruit. The Dempsey's love gardening. Roses and begonias fill the narrow beds of earth in their front garden. Their back garden, four times the size of the front, is filled with fruit trees that we eye enviously; apple, pear, plum, and peach.

Along the wall that separates our gardens are shards of glass sunk into rough cement. Mr. Dempsey is certain everyone's focused on stealing his fruit. His place is a bit like the Garden of Eden, all fruit trees and plants. Nobody is allowed over there, though. I never see his wife help out in the garden, but she's often down at the church, where she sweeps the altar and arranges flowers in vases.

We leave his property alone for the most part—the splintered bottles a perfect deterrent. Today however, we're emboldened by the absence of my parents, and Aunt Martha's snores fill the house.

The plan is to lay a plank across Mam's flowerbed up against the wall, take a run up the incline and spring into the lower branches of the apple tree. Once over we'll throw across the wall as many apples as possible.

Rock-paper-scissors, and I'm the advance scout. Its uneven sides wobble, and I take a deep breath and approach the platform. It's like being on a horse at the Dublin Horse Show, as it gallops toward the big wall in the Puissance: ready to leap.

The plank slips, despite Tommy having anchored it on one side, and momentarily unbalanced, I fall forward. I reach out my hands to stop my head from hitting the wall and my right arm slams onto the shards of glass. A flap of flesh hangs from my forearm and the blood splatters all over the wall.

Tommy takes one look at me and flees, town crier to the world. His yells awaken Auntie Martha who rushes into the kitchen. I hold my torn left arm out to her, not overly worried at the sight of the bloody mess and quite calmly ask for a bandage.

"Jesus, Mary and Joseph! What have you done?"

"I fell on the wall and cut my arm. It's okay. Put an Elastoplast on it and I'll have a big scab in a few days."

She runs to the kitchen drawer to find a tea towel to wrap around my arm. I'm shepherded across the road to our neighbor, Dan O'Malley's house. His wife, Bridget, is a registered nurse and she takes one look at my arm and dials 9-9-9 for an ambulance. I'm near to fainting from loss of blood and she sits me down on a chair in her kitchen while we wait for the ambulance. When it hasn't arrived after twenty minutes she hurries me out to their Mercedes Benz and bundles me into the back.

Mr. O'Malley smells of cigars and whiskey, wealth and power. I've never been in such a posh car before, and the leather interior is amazing. We head off for the hospital, me waving at my poor Aunt Martha and the cluster of nosey neighbors who have gathered on the street.

As the car speeds along I can feel the pain in my arm where the glass tore the skin. The tea towel is saturated with blood and I try to look away. Poor Aunt Martha nearly passed out when I showed her the cut. I hope they can fix my arm quickly so I can play in the school soccer trials next week.

Mam and the Old Man arrive at the hospital, right as the doctors are about to wheel me in to the operating theatre. One doctor tells Mam and the Old Man they are afraid there are severed nerves in my arm and they need to operate immediately. They are quiet as the surgeon explains the procedure. I'm in a blue gown, and my arm is wrapped loosely in white bandages. Mam kisses me on the forehead and says it's all going to be all right.

When I wake up in the recovery room, I hear the argument. Mam turns to the Old Man and says; "You'd better fix that man and his bloody wall before I do!" Her cat's eye glasses underscore her sharp mood. "Look at the poor boy. He could have lost the arm for good." The Old Man shakes his head at me and says he'll put a stop to Dempsey's gallop.

I'm in the ward for three days to make sure the operation is successful and there's no infection in the wound. The nurses spoil me with extra fruit and ice cream, and when I go to the bathroom one of them holds my hand in case I fall and reinjure my arm.

I'm mortified when I take a bath, because the pretty nurse from Wexford has to sponge me all over, and I'm embarrassed when she sees my penis with its few hairs. She's great though, and says to not worry, she's seen it all in her time as a nurse and that I'm not to be worried about her seeing me naked at all.

Mam comes to see about me while I'm there. She talks to the nurse who checks my bandages, and Mam winces in pain. "God, this one inside me is kicking like a donkey," she says.

"When are you due, then?" the nurse asks.

"November the 20th," Mam says, and pats my hand. I'm discharged on the fourth day and go home in the Austin Wolseley. The Old Man insists on driving and the car is still manky: ripped upholstery, stained roof where the rain leaks through. This is his first time on the road since the accident and he honks the horn impatiently and curses at strangers.

My arm is held together with twenty-eight stitches and the guarantee of a scar for life. We stop at Hector Gray's, a knick-knack shop on the North side of the city, and Mam buys me an Airfix model of a B-52 bomber. We drive the four miles home in silence, and I am ushered to bed the minute we're in the door.

Aunt Martha has fled to Athleague. Mam won't say why she's not here anymore, except that something came up and she had to leave.

Back at school my friends all want to see the scar, and I charge them a penny a look at the zigzag stitches. I'm the first one of us with proper stitches, and the oohs and aahs lasts for weeks. I jealously glance at the crimson plums in Dempsey's back garden as they ripen in the late-autumn days, and try to figure out how soon it'll be before I can climb the new wall and steal the forbidden fruit.

Halloween arrives. *Samhain*. The pagan feast of the dead. All over Dublin bonfires are being built from car tires, shopping carts, old sofas, and other debris. Bonfires, sparklers, and bangers become our focus. Tommy and I construct a giant mound of wood up the top of the lane beside the plant hire company's property. We collect broken furniture, tree limbs, and cardboard boxes—anything that might burn. By Halloween night the pile is ten feet high.

Last year in Ballymun flats some knackers murdered a donkey and stuck it on top of the bonfire and the smell had the locals housebound for days. Around our street it's quiet, but we've got big plans for some fireworks we bought off the street vendors in Moore Street last weekend.

During the year, we play Knocking Dolly. We ring doorbells, run away, and watch the people who answer try and figure out what's going on, and at Halloween we go one step further and stick bangers in letterboxes and run off before they explode.

Young boys and girls dress up in costume and go door-to-door asking the adults to, "Help the Halloween Party." Loose candy, Brazil nuts, almonds, monkey nuts, fruit, licorice, all end up in plastic bags, as brothers and sisters and friends walk around the neighborhoods in an assortment of costumes: witches, werewolves, ghosts, fairies, pirates, robots, even a few leprechauns with battered pots of yellow-painted aluminum foil.

When the streetlights come on it's the turn of the older children to enjoy the night. That's when the fireworks appear. Bangers are the number one choice of weapon: five inches long and thin as pencils, they make an almighty explosion when set off. More than one kid has lost a digit thanks to a faulty fuse or a fumbled safety match. Made in China; no guarantee of quality control.

We gather at the bonfire and dance around, jumping in and out as the flames lick their way up towards the wires on the telephone posts overhead. Bottles of cider stolen from cupboards appear, and we all take swigs from the brown glass containers.

"He fancies you Siobhán," Tommy says to a girl I don't recognize.

"Ah no. Siobhán your knickers your mother's coming!" Insults and comments fly like sparks from the fire.

We have bags of fruit and candy and a stolen bottle of gin from some house where the half-blind woman who answered the door didn't see Tommy sneak behind her into the kitchen and steal twenty pounds from her purse. Her old-age pension. The bastard. He crept out through her back door.

Tommy is thrilled with the gin and is already looped, yowling about Dempsey and how he'll, "show him who's the boss." The fires are too high; the electricity lines singe and snap. The lights go out in the neighborhood. It's crazy time.

"Come on then," Tommy shouts. "Let's get Dempsey." He has a mad glimmer in his eye.

Down the lane we run in the darkness. Tommy jumps over our low railings into Dempsey's garden path; wedges five bangers in the letterbox, lights the fuses, barrels back over the fence and slides behind a parked car and waits.

The first bang rattles the doorframe. The next four blow the silver letterbox out of the door. We fairly pee our pants laughing at the wreckage. The door opens and Dempsey appears with an antique rifle in his hands. It must be his gun from the 1916 Easter Rising.

"I know you're out there, you bloody cur. Come out and let me get a shot at you." Dempsey leaks spittle from his mouth and peers into the night.

Tommy is on the ground behind the car, howling. We stand in the shadows pressed against the wall of the lane, waiting for Dempsey to fire. It never comes. He yells for another five minutes and goes back inside, shutting the blackened and broken door. We head back to the bonfire in fits of laughter.

"Do you think he'd have shot me if he'd seen me?" he asks.

"Bloody well right," I say, "He wanted to blow your head off."

We snicker as we sit around the bonfire with the swinging electric wires showering sparks. Some older boys, along with what's left of the neighbor's gin, send around the cider bottles again. Then the ghost stories commence. Long into the Dublin night we sit around the reddening fire and tell stories of the Phooka and the Hellfire Club up the Dublin Mountains.

The next morning is a Saturday, and in the chill November drizzle we look at Dempsey's door. It's a sooty mess where the bangers have blown the letterbox out. At some point a squad car arrives and a policeman enters Dempsey's house and re-appears some twenty minutes later putting away his notebook.

Over at Tommy's house the policeman informs his mother how Dempsey saw Tommy in the streetlights that night.

"He saw him then?" she replies.

"Yes, Ma'am. So, he said. I have it here in my notebook." The guard licks the lead of the stubby pencil and waits to write in his book.

"Well, you can tell him from me he's a damn liar and he saw no one. He's trying to hurt my son. There was no electricity here last night and you couldn't see a thing at all. If he says he saw something he's mistaken." Tommy's mother purses her lips and waits for the guard to respond. Her face is brassy.

"I'll investigate that now," the guard says.

"Be sure yeh do. And the bangers? That's those feckin' buggers from Saint Enda's Road again. Those gurriers ran riot around here last year, but you were still in school yerself then." And that is that, as far as she's concerned.

"I'll get back to you if there's anything else, Ma'am," the guard says tipping the brim of his hat to her.

"Oh, you do that now son, you do that," she says.

Nothing ever comes of Dempsey's claims, and he put in a new letterbox, fireproofed this time. Tommy continues to tell the story of how he's blown the Dempsey door off its hinges, and at school he's known as "The Bomber."

Chapter 14

I walk up the avenue rattling a stick against the railings of the houses. There's a grate beside the electricity pole outside our house, and a familiar man pokes about in the mucky water and leaves that overflow from the rain. He's old, much older than the Old Man and he's got a huge white beard, and it looks as if he's wearing a lot of coats and jackets. Johnny Fortycoats, is his name, and sometimes we chase him up the street singing cruel songs.

I tell Mam about Fortycoats outside in the rain. She's in the kitchen about to baste the chicken. A load of giblets drips onto the cutting board. "Arrah, the poor man is bewildered." She drops the giblets in a pot of boiling water and lifts the naked bird from the counter. The bird's one eye stares at me, the beak open slightly. A sickening croak comes out of it and she drops it to the floor. "God forgive me, it's still alive," she says, grabbing my arm.

But it's not alive. The lumpy, featherless carcass is not moving at all. Mam takes it from the floor and dusts it off with a dishcloth.

"That's dirty," I say. "Father Donnelly in science class said our food should be sterile."

"Don't talk nonsense. My floors are spotless. The Queen could eat her dinner off them," she says.

I laugh at the idea of the Queen of England eating roast chicken in our kitchen.

"Go on, now. Get out from under my feet and go and play with your pals," she says, popping the chicken into the oven. "I'll call you for tea. God only knows what time your father will be back from town."

The Old Man went into the city this morning to see about unemployment claims or something. He's been gone all day, and the house is grand and quiet.

Tommy is hanging out at the battered gray Ford Anglia at the top of the lane. Birds nest in the hole where the engine used to be. We like to hang out in the torn seats, smoking cigarettes and imagining driving it down the lane and out onto the Rathgar Road.

The inside of the car is a magic carpet of empty beer and wine bottles, Tayto Cheese 'n Onion packets, and filthy rubber bags filled with snot. This stuff is stuck in between the pieces of upholstery and exposed springs. Tommy pokes a stick in the open petrol tank to see if there is anything there. The end of the branch is wet, sticky, and smells of petrol.

"Right then, give us it here," I say, grabbing the stick and wrapping a grimy cloth about it. "Give us the matches, too." I light one, hold it to the cloth and the yellow and red flame travels up the stick. I shove it into the tank of the car. Nothing much happens until thick black smoke billows out of the narrow neck of the petrol tank.

"It's probably going to explode," I say, knowledge gleaned from too many episodes of the new ITV police show, *The Sweeney*.

"Yeah, let's get out of here," Tommy says, legging it home.

We run towards his back garden where the tree house sits twelve feet off the ground in the limbs of a Sycamore. He has bottles of lemonade and bags of crisps we've nicked from the Dairy. As we guzzle Nash's Red Lemonade and crunch our crisps, smoke piles into the summer sky.

"Giz another bag of crisps," I say, and as I pop the air out of the crisp packet the tree shivers and we fall against the wall.

"The bleedin' car!" Tommy points at the flames now reaching high into the air.

"Holy Mother of God!" I say.

Out the window flowing sheets of orange ripple in the air. The smell of burning plastic is accompanied by the popping crack of empty bottles. We laugh and clink our lemonade bottles together in celebration.

"Nice one," he says. He slaps me on the back and I spray orange soda all over the place.

The flames still flicker in the sky and a scrawny tree next to the car is lit up like the burning bush from the Bible. High above, the flames engulf the telephone wires. A loud snap and the wires drop to the ground, the telephone pole blackened.

"We're dead," I say. "I'm heading home."

I take the shortcut up the side of the lane and out onto the avenue. Mam is on the telephone when I get inside. All I hear are the words, "Fire, car, and power lines." She hangs up the phone and asks me where I've been.

"Playing with Tommy in his tree house," I tell her.

"Don't tell fibs." She grasps my arm at the bicep and pulls me close. Through closed lips she says, "Did you two lads have anything to do with that fire? Did you?"

My eyes redden and my throat tightens. I squirm in her grasp.

"No, Mam. There was a tinker up the lane messing with the car, so Tommy and I ran off."

"Sacred Hour, I'll bloody well murder the pair of you if

you're telling lies." She takes the phone off the cradle and dials Tommy's house.

Her terse goodbye to Tommy's mother coincides with the "whee whaa" of a fire engine as it speeds up the avenue. It's far too wide to make it up the lane. The truck stops and four yellow-slickered men get out and begin to uncoil hoses. One of the men takes a crowbar and opens a grate on the road. He slides the metal plate onto the ground with a clang. The other men pull the hose to the opening, attach it to a pipe and run up the lane unraveling the hose.

A fire department car pulls up behind the truck and a man in a navy-blue uniform gets out, clipboard in hand. He walks to our garden gate and comes towards the door.

"Hello, Ma'am. Are you the woman who reported this fire?"

"I am, officer," Mam says. "My son here was playing in the lane when it happened." Mams arms are folded across her belly where my new brother or sister grows, preparing to come out any day now.

"I'll have a few questions for the boy if it's all right with you? Can we step into your house then?"

"Come into the dining room."

I gulp a breath down that hurts my neck and I watch as the man closes the door.

"Sit. Sit. Now son, you'd better tell me the whole story," he says.

And I do, the deep gold of his buttons impress me more than the hard look on his face. I tell him how we saw one of those tinkers at the car and how he lit a match and dropped it in the tank.

After twenty questions, I sign a sheet of paper and then he's off to see Tommy. Mam's offer of a cup of tea and some fig-roll biscuits is declined with a tip of the hat and he bids us a good day.

The white clouds of smoke fill the whole avenue, and the

stench of burning is everywhere. Coughing and spluttering, back down the lane rolling up the hose come the black-faced firemen. Mam brings out a tray of glasses and a pitcher of iced water to the street and the four firemen thank her for the kindness.

After the truck drives off she ushers me inside and closes the door. "What's that smell?" she asks. "Oh, Holy Mother of God, the chicken is ruined!" She dashes to the kitchen and with the oven mitts on, pulls the casserole dish out, the chicken, a burnt offering to a pagan god.

"Well, you ruined dinner," she says. "Up those stairs to your room me lad," she commands. "No dinner for you tonight. And I'm putting this in the ledger for your father to talk to you about when he's back from town."

Mam has her shopping bag and the list she wrote out after breakfast. It's the weekend and we get the 15B bus to town. The Old Man is staying home by the fire, afraid to get a chill in his gammy leg. Before we leave I put a shovel of slack on the coals and the moisture causes the fire to hiss and pop like Rice Krispies. I linger with the Old Man for a few minutes, not wanting to head out into the frosty Dublin morning, but when Mam tells me, I kiss him on the head and say goodbye. He gives me a smile and says, "You're to be a good boy and carry the messages for your mother. She's not able to lift anything too heavy in her condition."

There was an early freeze last night and the hedges on the road are white. Underfoot the ground crunches, and as we cross the road to the bus stop Mam slips and almost falls. She grabs hold of me and steadies herself. An old woman is waiting with a black West Highland terrier and when the dog whimpers she says, "Hush, Rommel, hush." Mam raises an eyebrow at the dog's name.

As we wait for the bus I watch Mam from beneath the

hood of my anorak. The line of her jaw is round and soft, and her hair is no longer perfectly permed. Now it is a tangle of moss-like gray because she's taking care of the Old Man. When she talks to her friends on the phone she uses the word "invalid." It means sickly, or unwell, but it also means not important anymore, and maybe that's how the Old Man feels now he cannot return to his job on the oilrig. She told Mrs. O'Malley his health was "delicate."

In Arnotts' Department Store she has me try on a new school uniform because I've grown so much recently. The jumper is scratchy and the polyester pants are full of static. She says I look "smashing," and we make a detour to have a cup of coffee in Bewley's on Grafton Street. I'm allowed get an angel cake with whipped cream and little wings sticking up from it.

The inside of Bewley's is like a ship stuck in a fog bank, and wreaths of smoke collect around the light fixtures. Mam's belly is huge, and she rests a glass ashtray on the edge of the table, smokes her cigarette and crushes the butt out.

The brass rail beside our table is shiny like a mirror and I use it to mess with the pimple on my chin. She slaps my hand away and says, "Leave your poor face alone. You've delicate skin and you shouldn't irritate it."

Chastened, I slurp my tea and eat the last of the cake. She beckons the waitress over with her "proper" accent, the one she uses when she speaks to people she considers her social inferiors. She thinks I don't notice, but I do.

We walk back across the Liffey, and in a corner by the Irish Times building a man is taking a pee. The stream is all the way across the footpath and she wrinkles her nose in disgust. I see the top of a beer bottle sticking out of the man's coat and ask her if he's an alcoholic. She shushes me and says, "God love the poor creature, he's addled with the drink. Sure, they get terrible treatment altogether."

I see another man slumped against the ground. Under

the raincoat is a familiar garment. It's the blind man we saw from the bus. He's dirtier now, the coat ragged and torn, and his white cane is nowhere to be seen. There's something about the way he's lying on the ground that reminds me of the Old Man on those afternoons he falls asleep in his chair, full of drink. What if he'd not married Mam and lost the business and my uncle hadn't helped him out with the mortgage money. Would he be lying in a gutter as helpless as this poor creature?

As Mam pulls at me I try to keep him in my sight, but we turn onto Aungier Street proper and I can't see him any longer. It takes forever for the bus to arrive, and when it does we climb to the upper deck and sit at the front. I can see right down into the space where the destination name goes and realize the bus is not in good condition at all. For the rest of the journey I grip the steel safety bar in front with both hands and don't let go.

We reach the lamppost outside our house and the sitting room lights are on. Through the window I can see the Old Man in his chair where we left him. Mam puts the key in the latch and shouts for him to wake up, and when he doesn't reply we go into the sitting room to find him wearing his oilrig gear, the kitbag by the chair, as if he's ready to head back to the North Sea at any moment. He's not snoring and Mam shakes him by the shoulder and his head falls to one side.

"Oh, Jesus, Ronan, you'll put the heart crossways in me," she says, shaking him again. I realize he's gone and take a step back from the chair.

"Oh, darling, no," Mam says, and starts weeping. The angel cake churns in my stomach and I want to get sick. "Son, would you go into O'Malley's and ask Daddy O'Malley to come over?" she asks.

I run next door and ring on their bell for a long time. When Daddy O'Malley answers, I say, "The Old Man's dead. Mam wants you to come over."

He rushes to get his coat and together we return to the house where Mam is wailing and shaking the Old Man, who is lifeless in the chair.

"Ah, Helen, come away, come away." Daddy O'Malley takes Mam's elbow and steers her to the kitchen. I'm left alone with the body. He looks as if he's fallen asleep, and his eyes are closed, his mouth slightly open.

"Da?" I push at his arm, but it's as if the muscles have left him. His head falls to the side of the armchair and I say, "Ah, stop kidding, Da. Wake up, would you? What's Mam going to do with a new baby on the way? You can't leave us like this." I wipe my nose with my cuff and the tears refuse to come.

The sun is out and through the curtains a long narrow ray lights the armchair. I leave the Old Man in the warm sunlight and go to the kitchen where Mam rocks in the chair, cradling her belly as if holding the baby inside her. Daddy O'Malley is making a pot of tea and he smiles at me.

"I'll phone Father McDaid for you, and then the funeral home. They'll want some clothes to put him in for the viewing," he says.

Mam gets up and says she'll root out his best suit and the old school tie he keeps in the wardrobe. I don't know how to behave with a dead body in the house, but remember Granny's funeral and tell Mam I'm sorry for her loss.

"Ah, God love you, Son. It's your loss as much as mine," she says. "We'll have to be strong now, especially for the new baby."

I'll have a week off school for the funeral. Kieran Boyce's mother died last year and he was absent for months. When he came back to class we treated him like he had some strange disease—Bereavement. I don't want to be treated that way at all. I don't really know how to feel because the Old Man is dead. I'm supposed to be sad, I know that. But he wasn't nice to me at all and he murdered DeValera. Still, he's my dad, and I should be feeling sad.

By evening, the neighbors start to arrive and with them they bring food and drink to beat the band. Mammy O'Malley comes in and helps clear space in the fridge for all the Tupperware containers and bowls filled with salads, pies, and roasts. Mam says people are too kind, but Daddy O'Malley says that's what neighbors are best for, when things go wrong.

We go around the rooms lowering the curtains and putting candles in the windows like we did when the Bird died. Mam and Mammy O'Malley eat croissants and wait for the priest to arrive.

"You'll be needing a check for the funeral home, too," she tells Mam. "I'm sure the oilrig will give you some bit of a pension, too."

By lunch the next day, Uncle Harry and Auntie Martha have arrived by train from Athleague, and they've brought platters of sandwiches from the local delicatessen. When Mam sees Harry, she bursts into tears and slumps into his arms. Right now, life feels like a science fiction film; the world moving far too fast, and completely disorienting me.

Uncle Harry helps Mam to her feet and hold onto her like she's a sack of potatoes. After a bit, they disappear upstairs to view the Old Man's body. He's going to lie in repose in the funeral home as soon as the undertaker brings him for embalming.

Uncle Harry takes me in his arms and gives me a bear hug. "Sorry about your da, he was a good man," he says.

I don't know whether to believe him or not, because I saw how they acted at Granny's funeral, and I could tell they didn't like each other one little bit.

Auntie Martha dabs at her cheeks with a handkerchief and says what a fine man he was. I'm leafing through the *Pears Encyclopedia* looking at a photo of the Bayeux Tapestry. William the Conqueror has an arrow through the eye and his horse is rearing up. Maybe it'd be better if the Old Man had died in battle, too. Instead he died in the sitting room, the newspaper on the racing page, his glasses on the carpet.

Bluebottle husks litter the ledge on my bedroom window. When the priest came around last night he anointed the Old Man with oils and gave him extreme unction even though he already departed. He also put his hands on Mam's belly and said a prayer for the baby's safe delivery. I ask what would happen the Old Man's soul if he wasn't anointed and the priest puts a large hand on my head and says I am not to worry.

Uncle Harry sits vigil with Aunt Martha and the Old Man's body, while the priest sits in the dining room eating coconut fingers and supping tea. I hide in my room, music playing softly on the record player. Jackson Browne's "The Pretender" is turning around and around, a persistent scratch as the needle catches a bit of dust.

Georgie Best smiles down from the poster on the wall, his moppet hair perfectly in place. I like the way his elbow sticks out because of the way he rests his hand on his hip. He's like a gunslinger; instead of shooting Indians and outlaws with guns he scores goals. I've lost my appetite and there's a bubble of sadness stuck inside me.

I peek into the room where the body is, and Auntie Martha holds the Old Man's dead hand and acts as his guardian before the undertaker arrives.

The doorbell rings and it's the Prendergast's arriving. Cathy hugs me tight. Her mother gives me a hug too and I can smell her perfume and it makes me feel all funny. I pull back before my excitement is too obvious. Mr. Prendergast shakes my hand and says, "We're all very sorry for your loss, young Patrick."

"How are you going to manage with the baby on the way and young Patrick still at school?" Mrs. Prendergast asks Mam.

She says, "I'll get the children's allowance for the two of them when the baby arrives, and there'll be a little bit from the oil company I suppose. Though, Patrick will have to leave school and get a trade."

When I hear this my knees turn wobbly and I fight back the tears. I don't want to leave school and become a trades-man. What about the university? Mam has always said I should go, particularly since she never had the chance herself because her dad, my granddad, died and left Mam to skivvy in the family business while Uncle Harry gallivanted about the countryside playing golf and racing his little Alfa Romeo. Why does the same thing that happened to Mam happen to me? Life isn't fair. Why did the Old Man have to go and die on us?

After a cup of tea and some cake the Prendergast's leave and Cathy whispers that she'll phone me in the morning. I smile at her and mouth a thank you. With the visitors gone I tell Mam I've got to go to bed. Upstairs, I try to find an answer to all the questions I have about the Old Man's death and what it'll mean for me, so I sit on the floor next to my bed and read "The Speckled Band," amazed again at how the murder took place. It's my favorite Sherlock Holmes story and I've already read it three times this week.

Mam says it's not normal to have unhealthy obsessions like reading the same books over and over, but that's what I like to do. She told me that I have to be the "Man of the Mouse," now the Old Man is dead, but that I'll be able to go to night school when I'm older and take the classes I'll have to miss when I leave school.

I don't want to be the "Man of the House." I want to be a teenager and do the things my friends will be doing. The pain in my chest hurts too much and I know I should go downstairs and say hello to the visitors who are coming in and out, and not be so selfish reading on my bed. It's what the "Man of the House," is supposed to do.

In the hall, a stranger is tapping his umbrella against the chrome hat stand and knocks snowflakes to the carpet. He's tall and skinny and has a drip on the end of his nose. When I say hello, he tells me he used work with the Old Man in the family business. I tell him my name and bring him to the kitchen where Mam speaks to him for a long time.

I'm bored so I go back upstairs to the anointed corpse. In the bedroom Auntie Martha snores, still holding the Old Man's hand, and Uncle Harry is asleep on the bed. Some vigil.

The undertakers arrive and four big fellows carry the Old Man's coffin down the stairs, scraping against the wallpaper, and out into the street where the shiny hearse waits. Mam screams and yells at them, telling them, "Wake him up! Wake him up! He's not dead. He's sleeping." The driver of the hearse rubs Mam's shoulders and lets her cry until they drive off to the funeral home.

The next day is the removal and I have to read from the Bible at Mass. I look out over the few dozen people gathered in the church, and finger the page with my reading on it and cough into the microphone, "A reading from the Letter of St. Paul to the Romans." As I pause before reading the lesson I see the stranger who spoke to Mam, wearing an ankle-length leather overcoat, positioned inside the doors of the church, collar turned up, dark glasses covering his eyes. His head is bowed, and he stands underneath one of the stained-glass Stations of the Cross. Via Crucis. Number VII: Jesus falls a second time. In the green, red, yellow glass representation of the fallen Christ the sun dazzles me.

The words come out of my mouth, and the people in the congregation take on a new shape and dimension. Perhaps some of them never knew the Old Man and are simply here for their daily dose of Mass–diligent Catholics, good folk–sinners on the path to redemption.

I finish my reading and return to the pew where Mam is weeping into her linen handkerchief. The priest goes through the remainder of the funeral mass at a fast clip. He says a few words, platitudes, and it's clear he never knew the Old Man at all.

Mam struggles after the coffin like a lost bird and I follow in her wake. The priest splashes holy water on the coffin and the undertaker's men wheel it down the center aisle. The priest takes long, slow strides, splashing more holy water on the wood. There's a miserable atmosphere in the church, and I can't wait to get out into the morning air and breathe.

The sun is trying to break through the clouds, and magpies are everywhere. It's as if they know a funeral is taking place and they've come to grace it with their presence.

The pallbearers slide the coffin into the back of the shiny hearse. Mam rests her head against my chest and I rub her shoulder. We're alone now, left behind by the Old Man who's gone to his eternal reward.

"That was lovely," an old woman tells me. "And be sure to help your poor mammy with the new baby."

I promise I will, and go after Mam once more.

After the formalities of shaking hands with the mourners is over, we follow the cortege on the long procession down to the family plot in Athleague. Mam dreads this part the most. The long drive into the Irish countryside, past the landmarks of her youth, as she takes this last journey with the man she loved for so long, who she'll never stop loving.

The cemetery is almost twenty-three miles from her hometown of Longford, and each town and road sign we pass is familiar to us, having recently driven this exact same route on the way to Granny's funeral. The landmarks we pass are not as recognizable to me as they are to Mam. The journey is a voyage into the past for her, into towns and villages now morphed into a collage of memories.

Rain falls as we pull off the road, the church on the right-hand-side—the last stop. Bleak, blustery wind flaps at the raincoats of the hearse-driver and his assistant. Two black crows on a gravel path.

Distant cousins and old customers of the Old Man who've been waiting under the eaves of the church come up to us in the parking lot. They shake hands and rueful heads, bemoaning our loss. Plenty of them say things about the baby, and how at least Mam will have the two of us to remind her of him. She snorts into a handkerchief and shakes her head.

Not many of the people assembled at the church are familiar to me, but Mam knows their faces and nods to one or two of them, her glasses spotted with raindrops. I hand her a fresh handkerchief, and when I take it back from her I notice the same man in the leather overcoat standing under an oak over by the low wall that surrounds the church grounds.

How many of these people read the Old Man's obituary in the newspaper? Any time he was home he'd make sure to keep up to date with who had died around the place. He read the obituary column every single day. First thing, even before the headlines. He always knew some old acquaintance in the listing.

"Ah, Love," he'd say to Mam, "Martin Doyle is dead. The poor hoor."

That's one thing you could say about him, he always acknowledged the passing of some acquaintance or other by sending a card to the widow and the bereaved family members. Mam and I are going to have to read all the cards and notes from people and reply to them. I won't know what to write to these strangers who all knew the Old Man somehow.

I meet with Uncle Harry and two other older relatives and agree on positions for carrying the coffin. Two of the undertakers are to assist us. I take my spot at the back right of the coffin. Around us umbrellas unfurl like black mushrooms and people take off their hats as we plod up the muddied hillside to the open grave.

My shoes slip on the slick grass, and I hope I don't take a header and have the coffin crush me. My shoulder hurts from where the coffin digs into it, and I see the undertakers have folded their black scarves and used them to cushion the weight. We trudge onward, step-by-step, past lined faces, men wringing tweed caps in their hands, women with mute-colored scarves wound about their necks.

Graveside, the coffin gets lowered onto a tarpaulin, three thick lengths of rope beneath it to play out and consign him into the earth. The priest, Stuttering Father Fitzpatrick, Mam's third cousin, three years before the murder charge that will see him excommunicated, blesses the coffin with holy water, the spills of rain diluting the sacred fluid. We make the sign of the cross and bow our heads. When the sprinkling is done, the six of us grasp the ends of the ropes and lift the coffin off the sheet.

"Down gently, lads. Easy does it," one of the pallbearers says. The rope slips in his hand and one side dips. The undertaker gives the nod.

Bear up.

Hold to the now.

Right.

Down.

Down into the maw.

When the coffin hits the bottom, the men pull the ropes out and the priest drops some soil on the lid and gestures at Mam to do the same. She peels off a black leather glove and fills a fist with wet clay from the pile beside the grave.

"Ah, Ronan. Don't leave me," she whispers. "Come on,

Son, say a prayer for the Old Man and your new brother or sister." She presses some of the soil into my hand. "Our Father..." she begins. She pauses and waits for me to join in. As I mouth the words, the soil rattles on wood.

We step back from the graveside.

Mam breaks down and cries out, "Oh Ronan! Don't leave me."

I slip my arm around her and keep hold.

I squeeze her tight, and she shudders. I know from her shaking that she's already crying again.

Mam weeps into her lace handkerchief, the rain sleeting angular, the crows beading the makeshift village of umbrellas crowded about the graveside. The priest crosses the air and mutters the prayers for the dead.

I hold Mam's hand, my feet squelching in the wet shoes, as the box inches its way into the dark. Over and over I repeat "One potato, two potato, three potato, four..." trying to choose which of the old people around the grave will be the next to die.

Finally, we turn in the direction of the car park.

"Come on, Son. Let's go home. It's you and me now until the baby arrives," Mam says, unfurling the umbrella as we plod along the gravel footpath that runs between the neat rows of headstones.

In the car park, the last of the mourners come by to say a few words of comfort.

"You don't know me, but..."

"He was a great man. God bless him."

"There's not many like him left."

"Sure, you'll have the children to remind you of him."

"Sorry for your troubles, Ma'am."

And then there are none.

All his family dead and buried.

A generation silenced.

"Five potato, six potato, seven potato more," I say, my eyes landing on a small boy riding his bicycle out on the road.

A crow caws from the church gutter and the rain pelts down.

The drive back to Dublin is miserable, the sky black as darkest felt. Already, I miss the Old Man, and how when we'd drive through Athleague he'd yell out, "Hurrah for shite," at the top of his lungs. Mam would always give out to him for the outburst. Now, she sits mute in the front seat with the driver from the funeral home. When he turns onto the avenue and pulls up outside the house, the candles we lit the night before still flicker in the windows.

We get out of the car and go into the house, where I put the kettle on for Mam, and let her climb the stairs to the empty bedroom, a glass of whiskey in her hand. I'm in the sitting room, the light shining on the antimacassar stained by the Old Man's Brylcreem. I know I can't bring back the dead; not Granny, nor DeValera, nor the Old Man, cold and alone on an empty hillside graveyard. I curl up and bury my face in his armchair, and breathe in the scent of his hair oil.

The heart inside my chest weighs a ton and I'm afraid it's going to sink to the bottom of my feet. How am I going to finish school now, and how is Mam going to make ends meet with a baby about to arrive? I've got no answers to these questions. Nothing is fair. There's no point in praying to God for help, because the Old Man is underground and God can't do anything to bring him back.

None of my friends knew what to say. Cathy and her family were at the church, but she didn't come up to me and just waved as they left for their car. Tommy punched me in the arm and went off with his sisters and mother. I suppose I'm alone now, alone and the Man of the House seeing as the Old Man is dead. I can't leave school until I finish my Inter Cert exams next summer, so between now and then I'll have to get a part-time job someplace.

The house smells like him, all Old Spice and Woodbine smoke. His fishing hat is on the rack by the front door, his pea coat hanging next to it. I unhook the coat and take it to my bedroom where I spread it on my bed like a blanket.

The kettle boils and I make a pot of tea and bring it up to Mam. She's sitting on the bed, holding a photo of the Old Man and crying. When I ask her if there's anything I can do, she tries to smile, but instead howls in anguish. We hug, her shaking body cold from the car journey. I stay with her while she drinks her tea and then she lies on top of the bed and is asleep in minutes.

I take a seashell from the top of my dresser and put it against my ear so the crashing waves can bring me back to the summer holidays in Mulrany. The skull I found at the end of the field perches on the dresser. The bright light from the street illuminates the eye-sockets, bringing the dead sheep back to life. I wrap myself in his pea coat and close my eyes. Next door, Mam and the unborn baby sleep.

Excerpts from the novel have appeared in various iterations at the following publications

Thrice Fiction Magazine
Connotation Press
The Drum Literary Magazine
WordPlaySound
Extract(s)
Gone Lawn
Scissor & Spackle
Drunk Monkeys
Orion Headless
Bicycle Review
Monarch Review
4'33"
NAP Magazine
Wordlegs
Red Fez
A-Minor
Cobalt Review
Literary Orphans
L'Allure des Mots
Daddy Cool Anthology
Tampa Review
Salt Magazine
Marco Polo
Shale
Camroc Press
Flash Frontier
Redactions
A Baker's Dozen
Nib
Tuck Magazine
Metazen

This book wouldn't exist without the support of my wife, Maureen, who steadfastly supports my creative life.

Heartfelt thanks to Ronlyn Domingue for her sage advice and editing, and to RW Spryszak and Dave Simmer II for all the support and work in bringing the book to publication.

*Much of this book had its genesis in the pages of both **Thrice Fiction** and **Connotation Press** and, in particular, thanks to Meg Tuite's tireless support of my writing.*

I'm also grateful for spending my formative years growing up in the Dublin suburbs; a place that to this day shapes me as a writer and a person.

www.ingramcontent.com/pod-product-compliance
Lightning Source LLC
Chambersburg PA
CBHW020117180626
46812CB00006B/2635